RASS

RASS

by Berniece Rabe

THOMAS NELSON INC.
Nashville / Camden / New York

Copyright © 1973 by Berniece Rabe

All rights reserved under International and Pan-American Conventions. Published in Nashville, Tennessee, by Thomas Nelson Inc. and simultaneously in Don Mills, Ontario, by Thomas Nelson & Sons (Canada) Limited. Manufactured in the United States of America.

Third Printing

The lyrics appearing on p. 131 are from "Wah-hoo" by Cliff Friend. Copyright © 1936 by Chappell & Co., Inc. Copyright renewed. Used by permission of Chappell & Co., Inc.

Library of Congress Cataloging in Publication Data

Rabe, Berniece.
    Rass.

    SUMMARY: Chronicles a young boy's continuing conflict with his father while growing up on a Missouri farm during the Depression.

    [1. Fathers and sons—Fiction. 2. Farm life— Fiction] I. Title.
PZ7.R105Ras3   [Fic]   72–13013
ISBN 0–8407–6284–4

For my sons—
Alan, Brian, and Clay Rabe

RASS

Preface

Not a lot of things of great magnitude happened on a share-cropper's farm in southeast Missouri in the late thirties, but the people loved to talk. Therefore, the things that did happen were told and retold.

Shoo away a chicken and brush off a clean spot under the catalpa tree and listen with me.

Hear?

They are telling about Rass. That is not unusual, for, as a rule Rass supplied more to talk about than the other children in this large family. Like one of the wild horses Dad bought cheap out west and then broke to the plow, Rass chomped at the bit to be free.

Dad was proud of the horses he broke in to do his bidding, and Rass wanted nothing more than that Dad should be proud of him, too. Trouble was, he was no horse.

One

There they sat, every one of them eating rapidly except Rass. He would never eat something that he didn't like, and no one could make him! He sat, barely watching, with his large eyes half shut and his bleached-out hair blowing like an old dandelion pod, just poking his fork in the hole in the worn red-and-white-checkered oilcloth that covered the big plank table. He looked at Dad, who sat in the place to Mom's right on the best cane-bottom chair. It was summer again, and Dad's long, work-toughened hands were so brown they were almost black. Rass feared those hands, but at the moment he was fascinated by their wrinkles and callouses and the darkness of them. They had got that way from working in the sun, just as he had got his own deep tan chopping cotton, when he had to, and hanging out around the ditches fishing while the sun beat the heat into him.

Dad was pretty old, even older than thirty-five. It was always "honor Dad," because of Dad's being "older and your father." Why did Dad still insist that Mom fry pork and put it on at every meal when they had had to eat the stuff all winter long? Things were done according to Dad's ways. Things ought to go other folks' ways once in a while. Dad had had his way about the side pork, but this cabbage . . . No, sir!

Mom looked at Rass and the rest of her family with a pleased smile on her big, smooth, stove-flushed face and said, "Won't be long till the chickens will be big enough to kill. In the meantime you can be satisfied with the change the garden stuff offers."

So far there had been radishes, lettuce, green beans, and onions. Now the cabbages were ready. Mom declared the heads were so big that just three of them would fill a wash-tub. She was right, and that was bad.

Rass wished now that he had stepped on every little cab-bage plant after they had set them out. He and the little girls had had to go along the rows of holes Mom had made and either drop in a cabbage plant or a dipper of water, whichever they had been assigned to do, and he had had the thought then but not the nerve. It was a shame he had not stepped on the cabbages, for he was ten now and should not have been a coward about doing it. He hated cabbage!

Dinner and supper for the past two weeks had been either green beans and cabbage, *or* potatoes and cabbage, and the usual side pork. Well, yesterday he had taken a bite of cabbage and almost knocked a door off the sideboard as he made a dash outside to vomit. Mom had thought he was really sick, but Dad had known what was ailing him. Dad had the power to know lots of things without being told.

Rass had screamed, "I hate cabbage!"

Dad had let him off with a shaking and a warning to eat what was put before him.

Today at the table Rass looked at the four little girls, sitting wide-eyed waiting to see if he would vomit again. On the other side of the table with Dad sat his big brothers, Willis, Frank, and Howard, smiles leaping about on their faces as they glanced in his direction.

Everybody *sat* at this table except Rass. Mom sat at one end next to the two-gallon milk crock, and L.G., his best friend and worst enemy, just two years older than he, sat at the other end. L.G. owned two barn cats, while Rass didn't have a single pet of his own. Rass *stood* next to L.G.

When Mom had decided that little Mary was big enough to leave her lap and join Sally, Roselee, and Sissy on the wooden bench on the right, she had shoved Rass off the bench around to the end with L.G. There was no chair for him. Dad had told him to sit on the hundred-pound lard can, but that meant he had to drag it from the kitchen each time and squeeze it past the sideboard and the table leg. So he stood up to eat. Oh, sometimes, when Mom was busy talking, Rass would swing out the lower door of her sideboard and straddle that while he ate.

Today Rass did not bother with the door. He had some planning to do. Dad would be on him immediately if he tried to pull the same stunt as yesterday. He reached across the table and got the cracked bowl that held the potatoes and served himself a man-sized portion. Maybe Dad could make him wear bib-overalls while L.G. wore jeans, and maybe Mom could make him swallow raw eggs to fill out, but cabbage? No! They couldn't make him eat cabbage again!

Dad said with deliberated calmness, "Will somebody pass Rass the cabbage?"

Three sets of hands reached for the cabbage bowl and passed it on down to him. He noticed that Willis did not help. Willis was bigger and stronger than both Frank and Howard, and much bigger than L.G., and could have been really mean to Rass if he chose, but he never was. He saw Dad's gray-blue eyes, steel-cold, and his weatherbeaten face dare him to disobey. He took out just a small amount of cabbage and went on eating potatoes.

Dad stopped watching him and busied himself with orders

to the older boys about chores. Dad always changed the subject as soon as he felt he had done his duty.

Quickly, Rass took some cabbage from his plate with his fingers and stuck it inside the sideboard behind him, where Mom had some canned goods stored. It would be no problem at all to come into the house in the middle of the afternoon for a cold biscuit off the top shelf of the sideboard and reach down, retrieve the cabbage, and scurry outside with it.

For over a week Rass was successful in hiding the cabbage in the sideboard. Then one night Mom made cornbread with cracklings. When she made that kind of cornbread she always started talking about when she used to be a girl. The little pulse in the hollow of her reddened neck would beat faster, her roughened lips would soften, and she would look off into space and think and chew the cracklings. When she did that now, Rass felt it was as good a time as any to hide the cabbage. Unfortunately, Mom was staring in the direction of the sideboard. She jumped up from the table and moved her heavy body around all those chairs in record time. She grabbed Rass by the seat of his pants and hauled him to the back porch. He still had cabbage dripping from his hand for all the family to see.

No woman had the right to pick a boy up bodily, Rass thought. No woman. Mom's whole face was red now, not just the usual red cheeks, but forehead and nose as well. She said, "It's a sin to waste food. And it's a sin to outsmart your parents!"

Dad said, "Now, you march right out to the peach tree and bring me in a switch! If it's a little one I'll wear it out on you and then send you back for another."

Getting his own switch! Dad meant him to hurt inside as well as out.

Rass came back with the switch, and Dad grabbed it and gave him the thrashing. Huge welts began to rise on his legs. So he went out to his private place, the chickenhouse, to think, and sat and watched the welts increase in size and redness. He didn't cry. He was a boy.

Sally stuck her head through the narrow chickenhouse door. "Why'd you do it, Rass?"

"I ain't eatin' cabbage. You jist watch! I ain't ever doin' nothin' that I don't think's right. See this welt, and this'n. Dad don't care how big they are."

Sally said nothing. Why didn't she leave? He hurt.

"Dad don't care for the likes of me and I don't care for the likes of him. I'll hate him until I die. He cain't stop that. I'll never like him!"

"Y'got to, Rass, or you'll go to hell. Y'got to honor your parents!"

"Not until he honors me!"

Sally paused and then asked, "What does it mean, honor?"

"Well, like, I guess."

"Then you got to be thinkin' on how y'can made Dad like you," she said.

"Dad won't ever like me unless he jist wonts to and I don't reckon he'll ever wont to, and if I have to eat cabbage to git him to wont to . . . well, I ain't!"

"Dad's wontin' to ain't it, Rass. Y'gotta do something great so that he'll have to like you, or you could be real funny or real sick. Mrs. Brown honors Bill a lot 'cause he's deaf and dumb. Or maybe y'can catch a big fish like Dad did when he was a boy and get famous, just like Dad!"

"Sally, I'll do my own thinkin'," he said, and made a paste of dust and smeared it on the welts.

He was not likely to be sick, he thought. He never had been, and folks didn't do great things unless it was an accident, and that couldn't be planned. As for being funny, well, Dad never laughed.

Sally said, "Next time why don't you *ask* Dad to use a switch, and then he'll use the strop for sure. Strops don't leave sich large welts."

Rass never took advice from girls, least of all Sally. She was two years younger than he was! Still, her words stayed with him when she left.

The next day all eyes were on him again, waiting to see if he would eat cabbage. He did not know what he was going to do. He only knew one thing and that was: he was not going to eat that rotten-tasting stuff!

Dad bowed his head, readying for the fight, and said from deep within, "Will someone please pass Rass the cabbage?"

The hands were a little slower this time. Rass's older brothers warned him with their eyes to go along with what Dad asked. He did not take any cabbage from the bowl, but set it to one side. Dad's top lip drew tight, relaxed, then tightened again as he rose from his chair and dipped a huge pile of cabbage onto Rass's plate.

"I ain't gonna eat this cabbage because it makes me puke!"

Mom got up and would have had him in seconds if Dad had not reached out a long arm and stopped her. The wrinkles that went down the sides of Dad's face deepened and his chin went up as he commanded, "Sit down, Mom. If the boy don't want to eat what you work so hard to fix, I guess he jist ain't hungry. He'll eat what the land provides. I ain't got money for fancy vittles for no spoiled kid. Leave the table, Rass, and I don't want to see you back here again until you're ready to eat like the rest of us."

Rass was not asking for store-bought food. Why did Dad have to be so mean? He would eat all the potatoes and beans the land provided. He said, "You don't eat eggplant!"

Roselee said, "Did Grandpa make you eat eggplant, Daddy?"

Sally said quickly, "I like cabbage."

"Let what you got to eat stop your mouth, girls," Mom said.

Rass went outside.

For the next four days he never showed up at the table.

"Rass, I'll swear you're carryin' this too far this time," L.G. warned.

"Don't you ever get hungry?" Roselee asked.

"You'll go to hell for sure, Rass, if y'don't do as Dad says," cautioned Sally.

"You're goin' to starve if y'don't mind us, Rass. Remember, the Lord says to obey your father and mother." Mom spoke sharply, but worry quivers were stirring the firmness in her jaw.

"Look, Rass, it's not worth it. You gotta go along with Dad. Someday when you're grown y'can eat what y'wont. Y'cain't keep on without eatin'," Willis pleaded.

"I ain't starvin'. I got my ways." Rass threw another rock at an old rooster that was slinking around under the grape arbor, eating green grapes and catching bugs.

When Mom came upstairs to wake the boys on the fifth day of Rass's fast, she tripped on the pot that sat between the paint-peeling rusty iron beds. As she started to right it, she

17

stopped short and said sharply, "Who used this pot last night?"

No one answered at first. Then Rass muttered, "I even git it for usin' a pot. What did y'put it here for if y'don't wont me to use it?"

Mom answered flatly, "I didn't ask for any of your back talk," as she left with the pot. In about ten minutes she was back upstairs. "You don't need to put them dirty pants back on, Rass. Put on the new ones with the holes in the knee; least they're clean." Mom was still boiling because he had cut the knees out of his new overalls. They had grated on his knees and did not feel natural, so he had had to cut them.

"What do I need clean pants on for?"

"You're going to the doctor with me and Dad," she said, and then she turned to L.G. "You can tote and fetch Grandpa's breakfast out to the little house for Rass," she said. "Tell Grandpa Rass'll be gone all mornin', and see to it that he don't set them pots of dirt right in front of the door agin. Git dressed, Rass."

Rass just stood there. The older boys started asking their mother questions. Everyone knew Dad's feelings about wasting money on doctors.

"It ain't nothin' to git excited about and it ain't none of your business. Now git on down and eat breakfast and don't ask any more questions," Mom said.

All the while Dad hitched up the horses to the wagon he grumbled about losing a half day's work in pretty weather. "Heaven only knows how long weather like this will last," he said.

Rass sat low in the wagon bed, watching his parents as they rode high and determined on the seat in front of him. Mom wore her gray-flowered dress, almost covered over by a large but clean ruffled wrap-around apron. Her hair was combed back into a gray-and-yellow knot. She looked big next to Dad. Dad had on his same old work overalls and worn, ragged jumper. The stoop of his shoulders, caused by plowing with spirited horses pulling the reins against him, was accentuated more than usual. He lifted his sweat-stained hat from time to time and wiped the white skin of his bald head, which never got a chance to get browned like his face.

They reached Doc Nitcheley's office in midmorning and found him asleep in his dentist's chair, for he was both doctor and dentist for the whole swampland section of southeast Missouri. Doc got up when they entered. "No rest for the wicked, they say. Come on in. I been up all night."

"Anyone we know, Doc?" Dad asked.

"Yes, ole lady Pratts. I gave 'em a statement to take her to the asylum at Farmington this morning. She's gettin' to be more'n I can handle." Dr. Nitcheley swished the tail of his soiled white cover coat aside and started to ease his broad bottom back down between the arms of the chair.

"We come to git you to check over Rass and tell us what's wrong with him," Dad said, not wasting any more time on gossip.

Dr. Nitcheley reached into a large glass jar and pulled out an inch-wide flat stick about six inches long. "Say, 'Ah'," he said. The doctor gazed down Rass's throat through a shiny round disk that covered up most of his baggy, bespectacled eyes.

Then the doctor threw the stick into a box near him and started probing around all Rass's ribs and back and stomach. "Mind tellin' me what you have noticed wrong with him at home?" Dr. Nitcheley asked.

While Mom told how he had not eaten for the last four

days and about his not liking cabbage and how they were teaching him a lesson, Rass looked around the room at all the little glass-fronted cabinets. In one was a display of old decayed teeth, in another, he guessed, there must have been a good five hundred bottles of pills, and in another was an old coin collection. He stopped looking when he heard Mom say, "And, Doc, now he's passin' blood."

The doctor let the stethoscope drop from his short fingers and looked squarely at Mom. "You sure it's blood?"

"He used the pot last night. I saw it with my own eyes," Mom said. Her face was grave and serious.

"Well, now, he don't appear to be sick, and a healthy lad like this could stand to skip a few meals. Then, again, blood in the stool is nothing to take lightly. You better bring in a sample of the stool tomorrow and let me check it," Dr. Nitcheley said.

The office call was over and the adults got up. As they rose, Rass saw Dr. Nitcheley's old face crack into a smile when he looked at the used swab board Rass had sticking over the edge of his hip pocket. "One stick is hardly enough to make anything out of, son," Dr. Nitcheley said, and he took three more out of the big glass jar and handed them to Rass.

Rass waited until his parents climbed into their places in the wagon and said, "What's going to happen to me? Am I gonna die?"

"You ain't gonna die, y'heard the doctor say y'was healthy," Dad said.

Rass let his mind leave Dad and the whole situation and gazed across the flat land. If it weren't for patches of woods, he guessed he could see until the earth turned round. When he spied the woods where Dad and his older brothers had been clearing, he knew he was home. He said, "We could've gone to Uncle Jake's and seen Dennis since we was already in town. It wouldn't have been more'n another mile's drive."

Dad said, "When I got a sick kid I go to a doctor and not to Jake's. Let him do the same. We wasn't hauling you around this mornin' for pure entertainment, Rass! Cut the talkin' and let's try to get a day's work in yet."

It was Mom who woke Rass the next morning. She looked angry. Her lips were taut and her eyes had a mad squint; her hair had not been combed and knotted for the day, so it bushed about her shoulders. Her bigness scared Rass. She grabbed him by the seat of his underpants and did not even wait for him to get decent before she hauled him down to the sideboard. "No use lyin'! Did you eat that whole gallon jug of pickled beets I've been savin'?" she demanded.

He could have lied, but liars go to hell. He had been sneaking beets for four days. There was a difference between sneaking and lying.

Dad had been waiting for the answer. "Move, Rass, and let me at that phone!" he shouted. "I'll whale the daylights out of you later. I gotta call Dr. Nitcheley now and tell him we won't be in."

Rass stayed close to the phone to try and hear what Dr. Nitcheley had to say.

Mom was shouting at Dad, "You cain't call! Everyone on the party line will hear!"

"I ain't wastin' another half day of work to go tell a doctor my kid ate a gallon of beets. . . . Hello, Doc. We won't be comin' in with that sample you asked for. The kid's been eatin' pickled beets on the sly for four days."

"Good Lord," Rass heard the doctor thunder over the phone, "You're worse than a couple of newlyweds, bothering a busy doctor over nothing, and with that tribe of kids you got, too!" There was a pause. "Anyway, I wanted to mention that I did notice some tenderness in the boy's stomach. Nothing serious, mind you, but I'd hold off on foods that cause a lot of gas. Definitely no cabbage."

"Okay, Doc, Rass won't be fed no cabbage." Dad's voice was still sounding like the boss, but he knew who had won. He hung up the phone and grabbed for the razor strop, his anger too hot to allow time for a switch to be fetched.

So what was one whaling? Rass rubbed his fingers on the smooth wood of the sticks in his pocket. A boy had to keep his eye on results, not lickings! The results had been good because of Dr. Nitcheley. That was not a lasting sort of winning, but it was fine for the time being. He had known all along what the results would be; the only thing he hadn't known was how they would come about. At age ten, it seemed the hows were always chancy, but Willis said that things get less chancy as a guy grows up.

Best go out to the little house now, Rass thought, and see what it was that Grandpa was hollering for. Maybe he'd even help Grandpa with his experiments. It hadn't been a bad day so far.

Two

It was a wonderful time of the year. Not one potato bug was left, the cabbage had been turned into sauerkraut, the cotton was laid by, and there was a supply of firecrackers stashed back in the attic. To make things perfect, they were spending the Fourth of July with cousin Dennis.

Dennis was the only child of Aunt Katie and Dad's brother, Uncle Jake. He was L.G.'s age, and built short and stocky like L.G., too. Even so, Rass still liked Dennis. Dad didn't. Dad just never did like that lazy, happy, whittlin' type. Uncle Jake had more money than anybody else in the family, so Dennis always got everything he asked for, and he shared it with company.

Dad was complaining loudly about having to go. Mom was forcing everyone to take baths in the middle of the week, so that she could impress Dad's brother with a group of clean children. It was all worth it. Rass and L.G. had to haul three tubs of water out to heat in the sun, and then haul them in again, two to the smokehouse and one to the toilet, but it was little bother compared to what Rass had to do when company was to be at *his* house on the Fourth!

Mom yelled, "Rass an' L.G.! I don't aim to have to warn you again not to slosh out all that water! Now watch your step!"

The two had one of the tubs almost to the smokehouse

door. It was the one that looked shiny new inside because Mom had used it to make kraut. That was what cabbage was good for. Preacher Hoyt said that all things had a good side.

"Rass, lift your end! I cain't git it up these steps all by myself," L.G. scolded.

"Well, you give me the heaviest end! Why don't you stand on the ground and let me stand on the step and then see if you can lift the end-up level." Rass heaved harder on the tub handle. It came to rest on the top step. One more effort and they had it up to floor level. The floorboards were worn down to the hard grain, which made it rough, sliding a tub of water.

"Satisfied?" he asked, and a huge wave of water slurped over the side and rinsed the dust off his bare feet.

They centered the tub away from the slab of side pork that was still left and away from all the fresh canned goods Mom had already put up. That tub would be for Mom and Dad's private use. They set the next tub just inside the doorway so that Mom could stand on the ground when she washed the four little girls.

They then started toward the toilet with the tub of water to be shared by the boys of the family. Rass and L.G. would take their turn before Frank and Howard. Willis wasn't home anymore. He now had a wonderful job on a ranch out west, where he probably never ever had to take baths.

"Set it down. I got to rest my hands. Why in the dickens does Mom insist on havin' the toilet set so far from the house, anyway?" Rass set his end down, forcing L.G. to do the same. They both massaged the dent marks from their palms where the narrow handle had bitten in.

"I git to go in first!" L.G. said.

"Oh, no, you don't! I ain't warshin' in your dirt again! You never rinch off! I'll rassle you for it!"

He grabbed for L.G.'s knees and they rolled over in the dry dust and dirt of the path, then on into a patch of bitter weeds. L.G.'s knees came up under Rass's chin and the pain made him quick with the next hold, a half nelson. Muscles strained and dust was blown aside as their mouths were forced against the ground. L.G.'s face remained in the dirt for a few seconds before he came up again with a bloody nose. Rass had just laid a hard knee into L.G.'s stomach when they heard Mom.

"Git up from there this minute! L.G., rinch off and git your bath! Rass, you mind Mary, now that she's clean. A body cain't turn their back on you two!"

Rass hit the seat and knees of his pants a couple of brisk strokes, rubbed his arm muscle for a moment, and then shooed Mary upstairs. As soon as he was sure that Mom was through running in for clothes for the girls, he went to the hole in the attic and got out his firecrackers to count. Dad did not believe in wasting money on firecrackers. Rass wished he was out west with Willis earning big money. Even Frank and Howard had been allowed to hire out to chop cotton for money so that they could buy firecrackers, but he and L.G. had to stay home and work without pay. 'Course no one ever got paid for chopping at home. But the point was, a boy needed firecrackers on the Fourth of July!

Luckily an old hen had been hiding eggs under the corn-crib. Eggs were the same as money in town. Rass had crawled under the crib and found nineteen eggs. Then L.G. had caught him trying to wiggle back out and had had to give him assistance in return for a promise of a half share in the firecrackers. It had proved to be for the best, though, because

L.G. had also to swear to Dad that Rass had been home the whole afternoon when ole lady Moore called up to ask if Dad knew that Rass was toting eggs into town. Dad always believed L.G., and that came in handy at times.

Now Rass shoved the firecrackers back into the hole, turned Mary over to L.G., and went for his turn at the bath water. After rinsing off the worst dirt under the pump and getting a bucket of rinse water to take along to the toilet, he settled into the process of bathing.

Sitting there in the tub, Rass spotted a bit of orange color through a crack in the rise of the toilet seat. At first he thought it was a bright piece of paper but when he checked he saw that it was a huge orange-and-yellow spider! Really a giant! The head was a good three inches across and the body at least five inches long.

Rass jumped dripping wet into his dirty overalls and ran to the barn. "Frank, there's a giant orange spider in the toilet hole, this big!"

Frank said, "There ain't a spider in the whole world that big!"

"You're gettin' a little too old for that kind of imagination," Howard added, as unconcerned as a dried-up ditch.

Why bother telling Dad, if Frank and Howard thought he was lying? Rass ran into the house to get L.G.

"L.G., come out here and help me dig under the toilet! There's somethin' in the hole and I'm goin' to prove it to Frank and Howard!"

"Rass, I ain't about to dig under no toilet to prove nothin'! I jist got clean!"

"Hurry before it gits dark! Grab a shovel! I could tell Mom about you not rinching again," he threatened.

"I could tell Dad about the eggs too," L.G. said.

"You couldn't. Dad would take your firecrackers, too, if he knew. Now come on! I swear I saw a spider this big!"

L.G. came running out. "Well, why didn't y'say so in the first place?"

Mary tried to follow. "You move from this room and I'll spank you," Rass warned her.

They dug from the outside and after four shovelfuls of dirt, a beautiful orange-and-yellow snake uncoiled itself and crept out. A snake! Rass hit it on the neck with the point of the shovel, scooped it up, and started to the barn.

L.G. ran after him. "What kind is it? I never saw a snake like that!"

"How do I know? Sure is a beaut!"

They met Dad at the horse-lot gate. "Where in tarnation did you git that coral snake?" he screamed.

Frank and Howard came running.

Dad put on his reading glasses to examine it closer and explained how deadly it was, and his brows wrinkled when he heard that it had been found knotted up in the shape of a big spider in the toilet hole. Dad was impressed. Now there was a fact to be considered.

The little girls came running toward the barnyard with clean bare feet, Mary leading the way, and Mom clopping behind, yelling for them to stay out of the manure. It was a grand and serious moment. Rass had, without a doubt, saved the whole family from sudden death!

"That's not a coral snake; there's no coral snakes in Missouri," said Frank.

Dad took off his glasses and pointed them at Frank. "I'll thank you not to call me a liar! I've seen coral snakes and you ain't! Its a coral, all right."

"No," said Frank. "It's a scarlet king! The marks and color

27

are almost the same, except the coral has yellow on the outside edges of its black marks, and the scarlet king has yellow in the middle of its black marks. This one has it in the middle! It ain't poison at all.''

Frank need not think he could steal this important moment from him with a lot of fancy explanations! "It is *too* a deadly poison snake!" he yelled, and Dad nodded. For once Dad had agreed with him, and it had to be when they were both wrong. Frank knew facts and no one need dispute them—not even Grandpa would, and Grandpa just *loved* to argue! Frank could prove what he said. Rass should never have let him see the snake.

Dad cracked Rass across the seat and told him, "Git back and finish warshin' up. Look at the mess y'caused. Now all these girls got to be warshed over again. Git rid of that dead snake and start makin' amends!"

Dad was siding with a guy one minute and causing him trouble the next. He had been the one that started the idea that it was a coral snake, but for certain Rass would be the one to get teased about it. Somehow he would see to it that Dad got his share of trouble from the snake too. No one could argue against its being a pretty snake! Dennis would like to see it, too. Rass took it up to the attic and hid it in the bag with his firecrackers.

The next morning Rass was out in the barnyard by sunup, hitching the horses to the wagon, loading extra bales of hay for the girls to sit on, and hiding his scarlet-king snake and firecrackers under the seat out of Dad's sight.

Mom came out and spread quilts on the hay to protect the girls' starched dresses and started loading some food and a two-gallon pail of cream into the wagon. Dad came over and yanked the cream pail out again.

"Rass," he said, "take this back to the milk trough. Mom,

I'm tellin' you, they got cream enough to make the ice cream! Ain't it enough that we're totin' and payin' for the ice for them?" Dad's face was half hidden by his hat brim as he tried to hide his agitation.

Mom said, flat and certain. "I ain't goin' to be actin' like poor folks!"

"And why not?" Dad shouted. "We *are* poor! There ain't no shame in bein' poor! Now cut out this fussin' and load up the girls."

Mom should have known not to mention the matter of money when they were on their way to Uncle Jake's, of all places. Rass never let being poor bother him particularly, but he did not talk proudly about it the way Dad did at times. It was Grandpa who had the right idea, for he always planned and talked of ways to change poorness.

It took a while to get the entire family loaded, and the horses headed into town in the early daylight. Dad made Rass chase Ole Coalie, the dog, back home once while they waited, and then they had to go back again to load in more hay to keep the ice from melting. It looked like it was going to be a scorching-hot day, and there would not be a sliver of ice left by the time they had traveled from the icehouse to Uncle Jake's. The sun had already started to angle in across the still, wide, endless cotton fields. Cotton could be downright pretty when you did not have to be working in it.

The fields gradually gave way to the town, and soon they were at Dave's icehouse. Dad called, "Hey, Dave, give me fifty pounds and a sack of salt."

Ice! Oh, boy! Rass jumped out of the wagon, knocking Sally aside, and started punching around in the sawdust that covered the ice as well as the floor and the sides of the icehouse.

"Here's a fifty-pounder, already out," Dave called.

Frank grabbed the ice tongs from a rafter and hooked it around the huge cube and started loading it. Howard picked up a ten-pound sack of salt and threw it to L.G., who tossed it into the wagon, skimming the top of the sideboard by a mere quarter inch.

"Don't reckon I could harr out them boys o'yourn to hep me?" Dave asked as he took the money from Dad. Dave was quick to notice a body's work. Nice man.

Dad ordered Rass to sit down. Rass hesitated because he wanted to get near the ice. Mom reprimanded him. "Honor your father, Rass, like the Good Book says."

Rass began chipping off ice for everyone to suck on, and Mom said, "Be careful with that pick and don't give the girls but a tiny piece. I don't wont thur dresses wet."

Impatient, Sally stuck her hand in the way, and Rass nicked her. She screamed as if he had stabbed into her heart. He made a show of putting the pick away so Dad would not get his dander up again and occupied his time by staring Sally down and forcing her to cross her eyes when he pointed his finger at her. He hardly had time to finish off his hunk of ice and check his snake over good before Uncle Jake's huge, old, scroll-trimmed farmhouse came into view.

The house had thirteen rooms and must have once been a rich man's house. Dad claimed that Uncle Jake still thought it was. Rass could see Dennis running down the road to meet them and Uncle Jake's serge suit reflecting the sunlight as he stood in the front yard waiting. Aunt Katie was on the big-pillared front porch waving to them with a dish towel and pushing back the curls of her gray hair that always got un-ruly on a hot day.

Mom started showing her excitement by stretching the gathers, snapping, buttoning, creasing, smoothing, and pulling on the girls' puff-sleeve dresses. "You girls, smooth them skirts out soon as y'stand up. You boys, git your shirt-tails in so y'don't look so tacky. Rass, stop crawlin' under that seat. You'll have your pants knees filthy!" she scolded.

Dad's lips set hard, and he wiped the sweat from his head too many times. "They're farm folks, same as us," he said.

Rass leaped out of the wagon before it came to a full stop and went running toward the house. When he got to the high, worn hollow but still fancy porch steps, Aunt Katie caught him and kissed him. Dang bust it! He would have to remember to come in the back way next time. She couldn't keep her hands off a body, always patting, loving, straightening. She ought to just fuss over Dennis. Maybe someday Rass's own folks would make a fuss over him.

"Land's sakes, how these young'uns has growed! You must be feedin' 'em well," Uncle Jake said as he shrugged. Uncle Jake shrugged so often his stiff collars wore callouses on his ears.

Rass could not stand any more of the "hello talk," so he grabbed Dennis' hand and pulled him out back to show him his snake. "I plan on havin' us lots of fun with this here snake. Now, if one growed man would thank this is a coral snake, then another one ought to thank the same. Right? Let's put him down by the wellhouse and scare the waddin' outta Uncle Jake!" he told Dennis.

"I'll be a sonuvagun, Rass, that's the purttiest snake I ever laid eyes on! Don't look poison one bit," Dennis said as he stroked the dead snake.

Rass searched about the wellhouse for a suitable place for the snake. "Here's a good spot. I'll put him right next to these here rocks an' moss. Looks natural as all git out." He was pleased with the effect.

L.G. came up just then and said, "Too natural. Uncle Jake won't even notice it!"

"He's right, Rass. I know my own pa better'n either of you. I say put it over here by the cider barrel. Pa is gonna tap it today. Been savin' it for the Fourth," Dennis said.

Rass took the snake over to where the brown keg rested on a split log and placed it head up and around the spigot. Then they ambled in exaggerated innocence back to the house to help crank the ice-cream freezer.

Aunt Katie put the dasher down in the rich creamy liquid and locked the top on. Mom packed on more ice and salt and placed a potato sack on top.

"Sally and Roselee, you turn first till it gits too hard to turn; then the boys can take over," Mom said.

"Where's Uncle Jake?" asked Rass.

Mom said, "It's no concern o' yourn, and stay out of the men's way. Your Uncle Jake's taken Dad out to see the new tractor."

That was all right. Rass just didn't want Uncle Jake to go sneaking out to the wellhouse when he wasn't there to see the discovery.

He heard firecrackers going off at the back of the house. Must be Frank and Howard. Dennis heard them too and said, "While they're gittin' the first part of the crankin' done, let's shoot off some firecrackers. I got ten two-inchers, five candles, an' five blockbusters!"

As soon as they were past Mom's hearing, Rass whispered, "I got five one-inchers and three two-inchers, an' L.G. has the same, but find me a tin can and they'll *sound* like blockbusters! L.G., I'll try two one-inchers in the same can, and if it works, then you try three."

It worked, and the three worked even better. That can

went sailing in the air like a nighthawk. Boy, the Fourth of July was almost as good as Christmas!

"Hey, I know jist the thang!" Dennis said. He ran to get a small rusted teakettle with the top on it and wedged a corncob into the spout. If the lid had had a tail on it, you would have sworn it was a kite, it went so high. Too bad Dad could not appreciate such genius. If Dad *ever* appreciated anything at all, Rass would set off even more fireworks.

They finished the rest of his firecrackers before Dad returned. Dennis had saved two of his Roman candles and one blockbuster. He said he was waiting for just the right moment.

"Come on in and help turn," Sally called.

Rass gave Dennis a push and challenged him to race to the house. They raced nip and tuck until L.G. caught Rass by the galluses and slowed him up. He would settle with L.G. later, when it wasn't the Fourth.

The cream was soon so hard that Sally had to sit on top of the freezer to steady it while the boys took turns cranking. Rass's arm muscles ached, and he felt sure that if he turned just one more time the handle would break off in his hand.

"It's ready, Mom. I'm the last turner! I git the dasher!"

Aunt Katie removed the dasher and handed it to him. "Take it outside an y'all can git a lick, then come right in and eat dinner while the ice cream sets."

The plates on Aunt Katie's table were always turned upside down. Mom said it was the way things were done in Aunt Katie's family. Everyone sat down at the table and, like flying pages in a book, turned their plates right side up and started filling them with huge chunks of roast beef, peas, and the fancy fruit salad and French-fried potatoes that they never got at anyone else's house. It was nice to visit here.

Aunt Katie got up and returned with a stack of white saucers, looking as pretty as her stuffed divan with the white doilies. "Jake, help me scoop this ice cream. I do believe it's the solidest we've ever made. If you kids wont to eat yourn outside in the shade, you're welcome," she added. Aunt Katie sure knew how to be nice to children. It was uncommon.

Man, this sure was a good day! Rass had not felt the need to fight with L.G. but once, and he never counted the trips he made back in for refills. He never stopped until the ice-cream container was empty and Uncle Jake called, "Anyone want to go for a ride in the Chevy?"

Everyone was right there ready to go. Only Dad acted disinterested. Now why was he acting that way? Why, everybody liked cars!

The car was crowded with the nine children and two men, but it was fun breezing along so fast—past the cotton fields, over the drainage ditches, smelling the yellowtop and clover and looking across the miles of flat farmland in full growth.

Uncle Jake pointed out the good stand of cotton he had this year. "Look at the size of them squares! It'll make a bale to the acre. Mark my word!"

Dad must not have been interested, because he never answered, only scolded Sally for leaning out the car window. The dust billowed up from the dirt roads and coated their faces, but Rass did not mind.

When they returned, Mom did mind. "Git down to the wellhouse and warsh up! I never seen the likes of it!" Then she warned the girls, "Now be careful and don't mud up your dresses."

"Let's all go down to the wellhouse and crack the cider jug. It'd be a welcome cool," Uncle Jake said, and led the way.

The time had come! Oh, boy! Rass exchanged glances with

L.G. and Dennis, kicked some seed from a sour-dock plant, blew into his hands, and ran to be near Uncle Jake.

"It's kind of you to offer, Jake, and I thank you kindly," Dad said, "but me, nor my kids, take nothing similar to liquor." When Dad started using polite words it meant he was trying hard to keep from acting natural.

"I know it. I know you don't. But this ain't liquor. Now come on down and try it out," Uncle Jake said.

Dad said, "Okay, I'll taste it, but if it's hard we'll not drink it. My wife objects to liquor on Christian principles, and I object on the principle of what it does to a body, not to mention how cussed it can make a man in his old age. Take a look at Pa. I'll not have you be eggin' me on!"

It was true, as Dad said. Grandpa sure was cussed enough, and he drank. That was why Mom would not allow Grandpa to move in with them this spring when he was needing a place. But Dad had said that he felt duty-bound not to turn out an old man of ninety-four years, leastwise when it was his own pa, so he and Rass and the other boys had built a little one-room house out back for Grandpa to live in until he died.

Grandpa was sitting in it right now, waiting for them to come home and for Mom to make him some oyster stew. Grandpa's experiments would be forgotten today, for he would be drinking whiskey while they were gone. Uncle Tut, Dad's other brother, felt that he was helping take care of Grandpa by furnishing him with a bottle now and then, and there was no doubt, Uncle Tut's bottles were hard whiskey.

As they neared the wellhouse Rass pulled Dennis and L.G. back a ways. "Don't git too close, and don't let on none, or you'll spoil the show," he cautioned.

Uncle Jake stepped near the keg. "Yes, sir, I been jist

35

waitin' till you folks got—" His mouth moved without words, his eyes blinked as fast as his shoulders shrugged. "Move!" he yelled. "Run! Stand back! It's a coral snake! Stand back, now, everyone; stand back, hear?" As Uncle Jake's voice started to sound calmer, his legs began to move faster, and soon he was running wildly, pushing and pulling the children as he went, and calling to Aunt Katie as he neared the house. "Kate! There's a coral snake in the well-house, sure as God lives!"

Aunt Katie and Mom came running.

Uncle Jake kept talking. "No, I ain't stretchin' the truth. Never saw one in these parts befo——." It was fun to see Uncle Jake stop right in midsentence as Dennis held up the dead snake. L.G. and Dennis were howling with glee. But Rass waited to laugh until he saw what Dad did.

Dad looked at the snake. Then he looked right toward Rass and began to laugh. At first the laugh was short and crackling like a brush fire, but it grew to a bellow from deep inside. Dad was laughing!

Rass let his own laugh out now and did not stop until Dad took a good long breath and shouted, "Jake, cain't y'tell a innocent little ole scarlet king from a coral?" Dad held his stomach and doubled over beyond all reason. It was good to hear.

Rass had never seen Dad laugh so hard before, nor Mom get so angry. He had been sure Dad would give him a licking for bringing the snake along, but no, Dad was laughing about it instead.

Mom said, "Cut out that laughin'! Rass, your dad ought to be tannin' your hide instead of helpin' you poke fun! Y'd think after that stunt with the water moccasin last fall y'd know that snakes is serious business and not for joke pullin'." Mom pushed the girls back toward the house and made efforts to cheer Uncle Jake. Mom was mad. Well, she was not going to make him lose this happy moment!

Frank and Howard's "dead" water moccasin had sneaked away and nobody ever did find it again. Frank and Howard were fools. Rass had made certain that this scarlet-king snake was stone dead before he stuffed him in with his firecrackers.

"Well, reckon we better be headin' on home," Dad said finally. "Frank, go hitch up the horses. You kids, load in the wagon!" Dad's voice sounded normal enough, but Rass could see his sides still bouncing with laughter. Maybe this was the kind of joke Dad liked! Dad had never laughed at Rass's tricks before. A new, really good feeling encompassed him.

"There ain't no need rushin' off. Cain't y'stay?" asked Aunt Katie, but she was not looking at Dad or Mom. She stood stroking Uncle Jake as he sat in the porch swing.

Mom said, "Guess we better not. It'll be dark now before we git home and git the milkin' done and these young'uns in bed and settled down." Mom gave Dad a mean look and then gently put her hand out to Aunt Katie.

The wagon was full of family, so Rass quickly whispered to Dennis as he jumped on the end gate, "Gimme my snake."

Mom sat next to Dad on the wagon seat, but she seemed to be a distance from him, her back was so straight and stiff.

"You folks come see us," Mom called.

Everyone waved.

"And you'uns come back agin," Aunt Katie called.

Uncle Jake never said a single good-bye. He just started swinging hard and fast, back and forth, in the porch swing.

"Gitty up there, Nig. Haw, Jill!" Dad gave a rakish whip with the reins and the horses pulled out with a jerk. Why,

Dad was acting just as gay as if he were Willis driving Wild West horses! Rass said, "Wonder if that cider was hard." No one answered. All faces were set straight ahead, only the eyes were glancing first to Mom and then to Dad.

Finally, Mom pointed to a nice cotton patch. "Jake has a right nice stand of cotton," she said.

"Ought to have! On rich soil like this, he'd have to *plan* it to have otherwise!" Dad snapped.

Mom looked piqued. "Jake's a hard worker."

"An' tell me what farmer ain't! Bein' prosperous depends a lot on what kind of soil fate hands you." Dad gave the reins another gay flip and laid back his head and yelled, "Home, Nig! Home, Jill!" He twisted the reins around the wagon peg and relaxed. "Now I'd like to see a *car* take orders like them horses!" Guess there was no end to Dad's feeling fine! Suddenly his hand swept back and slapped Rass good-naturedly on the back. The long lines down the sides of his face split as laughter crossed them again. "Yep, Jake's shirttail never hit him till he reached the house! I never seen a little fat man run so fast since Santa 'most missed his sleigh!"

The little girls perked up at that and Dad started laughing again. Rass joined in. It was great to share a joke with Dad, man to man. A man! Whippee!

One thing was certain: Rass was not going to let this scene die out if he could help it. Guess he had just never realized before how much Dad liked jokes. At last he had found something that Dad showed appreciation for. Rass worked his way over near the wagon peg, eased off the reins, and coiled the snake around the peg.

The next time Dad reached to give the reins a pull, his hand jerked unexpectedly into the air with the snake dangling from it in all its beauty. Aw—oh! Dad's smile curled

38

into a snarl. He opened his hand to release the snake, then spread the fingers wide in a grabbing motion.

Rass fell over Frank and shoved L.G. aside as he jumped from the wagon to get away. Dad had hold of the reins and was drawing the horses to a stop. He would get him for sure.

Mom began laughing and said, "Rass is a good one at snake jokes! I don't hear you laughin', Dad."

Dad thundered, "Git back in this wagon, Rass! It's no time for a joke when we'll be late for milkin'." Then Dad turned to Mom and said, "I was jist thinkin of the time it's gettin' to be! That kid's got no sense, no sense at all about time."

Mom nodded and sat up straight again with a clear face and said evenly, "I'd like to stop off to see Missus Brown for a minute, about helping with the balers." Her sides shook with silent laughter.

Rass got back into the wagon. This *was* something, Mom laughing at one of his jokes! And right after her being so mad, too. All the children began to laugh.

Boom . . . boom . . . boom . . . boom! White, green, and red balls shot into the sky over Uncle Jake's place. Dennis had chosen the moment, a really big moment, to finish off the Fourth of July celebration. And there wasn't a soul in the wagon now who wasn't laughing, unless it was Dad, but Rass couldn't see Dad's face with his head turned away like it was.

Three

In the weeks that followed, Rass kept close watch on some horse hairs that he had in the watering tank, hoping they'd sprout heads and become snakes. Also he helped Grandpa with his experiments and listened to him tell his tales about collecting on his I.O.U.'s and reclaiming his lost land in Oklahoma and really getting oil this time now that he understood soils better.

Mom said Grandpa was old and addled, and Dad said it was a bunch of pipe dreams. Rass didn't set judgments. He just helped Grandpa when his other chores were done, or went out fishing or spent time playing with his new kittens, which he'd got from L.G.'s barn cat.

Still, at night, when he was too tired to work at reading his Zane Grey Westerns and making plans about running away to join Willis, he'd lie awake for a spell just staring at the tacks on the wallpaper. He saw himself riding the world's most vicious bull, or catching the world's largest fish, or being even richer than Mr. Pritse. It was a pleasant way to bide the time.

He needn't have worried about filling time, for they had to go to school for a whole month before they got out again for the cotton-picking vacation. But it gave him a chance to talk to Mr. Aaral, Frank's science teacher, about the horse hairs when they didn't take. He found out fast that Mr. Aaral could be a right nice person to talk to, and it helped him forget about snakes for a while.

Now he was back in the cotton fields feeling the burrs of the opened brown bolls prick his fingers as he raced to keep pace with L.G. so he could have someone to talk to. Truth was, he liked to talk, and not many people listened except for L.G. and Sally, and they each required a different kind of talk. He reserved yet another kind of talk for his kittens. It was a kind that took the place of dreaming, now that he was so tired from cotton picking when he went to bed.

Not everybody's cotton was well opened as yet, but Dad's was and Dad was getting it out fast before the price took a cent drop as usual. The hay crop had covered some of the bills but left little money toward thoughts of owning a car, and Dad had sold every bale he thought the stock could do without. Dad pushed the whole family hard, and no one dared rest unless it rained. It was raining today, and Rass sat by the window nodding to the drops as they slowly filtered down until Dad's voice swept in to distract him.

"I'm takin' the cotton load over to Malden today. They're payin' a cent more a pound. I stand to make fifteen dollars more by makin' the trip. It'll take a good portion of the day. No one is gonna git much pickin' done in the rain. L.G., you might as well ride along with me."

Sure, Dad wanted L.G. to ride along so they could talk car. Both of them liked that. Rass knew Dad wouldn't let him go along, but still he was thinking of asking when Dad added, "I'll haul them kittens off while I'm at it."

Rass remained sitting for a small flicker of time next to the window with his hand sticking out to catch the rain,

42

then suddenly slung the water from his hand in the direction of Dad. "Hey!" he yelled. "You cain't! No one is haulin' off my cats."

Instantly Dad's gray-blue eyes hardened, and he said, "Rass, one more word outta you and I'll give you a hard and firm thrashin' right here and now. I'll be lettin' you know that I'm the one what makes the decisions around here."

Dad could lick him all right. No matter if he *was* getting as old as dried pignuts, he was still tough as one too. Pox on a licking! Rass raced to the barn to be with his cats. He would not just sit and let Dad drown his pets. L.G. owned two cats, and they had no more right to live than his little kittens.

He opened the corncrib door, and L.G.'s big Old Tom walked out, leaving her three lively, skittering, unperturbed kittens behind her. They were scattering the loose kernels of corn across the bare parts of the floor. The pure white one with the softest pink nose leaped high into the air to box a spider from its web. It was the only one he'd named so far, and the name he had chosen would fit either a boy or a girl. He'd wait with the others until he was sure what sex they were. No one was going to catch him making the same mistake L.G. had made with Old Tom!

"Snowball, come here. Let that ole spider be. You're a smart one, even if y'ain't six weeks old yet. I'll bet you could catch a mouse." Rass held the kitten close, feeling the soft fur against his chin. "I ain't gonna let them take you off. I'll hide you." Rass felt comfortable talking to the kittens.

He knew better than to try to talk Dad into leaving them. He collected the three kittens and started out the door. Dad stood there blocking his way with a potato sack in his hand. Rass grabbed at the sack, but Dad held on, causing the dust and grain to billow back and choke them.

"Put them in here, Rass. Now round me up some string. I've known of cats comin' back for miles. These are too young, I believe, but there ain't no use takin' chances."

Rass made no effort to obey. Instead he heard himself plead, "Cats ain't no bother round the barn. Couldn't we keep 'em?"

Now why did he have to say that? The hurt screamed within him. He dared not cry. It was plumb shameful to beg when you already knew better.

"Hush up, Rass. You and the girls cut such a shine when I had to drown the last litter. You're ten years old. When are you gonna grow up? I'm doin' you a favor just haulin' them off to run wild instead of drownin' 'em."

"These here cats was never meant to be wild," Rass said, and he moved the black one in close to him so that Dad could not see it was sort of wild already.

"It don't pay to start likin' cats too much. Nur anything, far as that goes. Now git them in here. Time's a wastin'. This barn is swarmin' over with cats as it is," Dad said.

It was not only that Rass liked kittens, it was that these kittens also liked him, and that was important to know. It *did* pay to like kittens! But how could he convince Dad of that?

Anyway, the barn was not swarming with cats! There were only L.G.'s two Toms, Old Tom and Young Tom. Some people had as many as ten cats in their barns. He just had to keep talking in an effort to change Dad's mind.

"We could use a cat to keep the mice out of the house," he said.

Dad scooped the sack roughly against his arms, tumbling the kittens into it, and said, "We ain't bothered none with mice in the house. When you gonna learn I mean what I say?"

The empty feeling in Rass's arms threatened to engulf him, but he pushed it back in order to think out his next move. Dad grabbed a piece of baling wire from Nig's stall door and tied the sack shut, then walked to the high cotton wagon and threw it on top. The rain had slowed to a light mist now. Still, L.G. and Dad tied on the tarp. Gin managers did not like to receive wet loads of cotton. The tarp was cutting off any chance of Rass's ever retrieving his kittens. And if he didn't get on that wagon and save them, they'd most likely smother.

When Dad and L.G. jumped on top of the load, Rass ran like a rabbit, crouched under the wagon, and held tight, upside down, clinging to the long center coupling pole. The horses started with a jerk and moved on, with Ole Coalie Dog trotting behind until L.G. made him go home.

Rass did not mind hanging upside down. Sometimes, if he was bothered about something, he hung like that from a tree limb on a windy day or from a chicken-roost pole. His hair brushed the ground as he watched the wagon wheels go round. They seemed to be going backward. It made him dizzy. In order to rest his eyes, he quickly tried to focus them on the cotton that was pressed through the floor cracks. After a while, when his arms and legs gave out, he eased along toward the back and worked his way around to the end of the coupling pole that stuck out behind the wagon. He sat astraddle on it in comfort.

Now he could see everything that the wagon passed. Well, anyway, he would as soon as he had shut his eyes and allowed the blood to come to a rest in his head again in a right side-up way. Everything felt giddy and light, like after the rides at the carnival. He opened his eyes again and looked into the large liquid eyes of Ole Coalie.

"What are you doin' here?" he whispered. "Guess you don't take to bein' pushed around, neither, huh, Coalie?"

The wagon stopped. Rass slapped Ole Coalie and ordered him to hide. As Coalie slouched down in the road ditch, Rass peered around the corner of the wagon to see why Dad had stopped and saw a covey of quail slowly strutting across to the side of the road. They were almost at Number Five Ditch already. Wow, the water was low. A little rain was needed, all right, although nothing had stopped the burdocks from growing. They were high as bushes along the ditch dump. Finally the wagon started up again, and Rass and Ole Coalie got back into their former positions. No one had noticed them.

Rass counted off the ditches as they passed over them. It took fifteen minutes between ditches. There was one every mile. They crossed Four Ditch, then Three Ditch. He wondered what it would be like if there were no drainage ditches. Frank said it would be swampland, with water standing everywhere. Frank also claimed that a smart farmer could use land like this to grow rice if he controlled the flooding properly. Grandpa said Dad was a fool not to try rice growing, but Dad wouldn't. He said Frank was a fool.

"Whoa! Whoa! L.G., I thought you made that blame dog stay home. Git home, you black scoundrel!" A piece of green cotton boll came sailing over Rass's head.

Ole Coalie slouched into the road ditch again. "Better git home," Rass warned as he slipped himself back under the wagon. Dad was off the wagon now, pelting Ole Coalie with more cotton bolls. Coalie tucked his tail between his legs in submission and headed back down the road.

They had just passed over Number One Ditch when Dad headed the team south, drove a little way, and then stopped short of a farmhouse. Dad called, "Throw them cats off here, L.G.! Ain't no point takin' them into town."

Rass crawled under the wagon and watched as L.G. untied the sack and gently placed each kitten by the roadside. They were still alive! It surprised him that L.G. could hold anything so tenderly, because when he wrestled with Rass, L.G.'s hands were hard and rough and unmerciful.

The kittens must have been awfully cramped up and smothery in the sack, for they huddled close to each other and cried and sniffed at the strange ground. L.G. asked Dad, "Reckon they're big enough to catch field mice or young rabbits?"

"Things in the wild have to if they wont to live," Dad snapped, then cracked the whip, making the horses lunge forward.

Rass dropped noiselessly to the ground and lay there until the back wheels cleared him. Then he rolled into the shallow, freshly mowed, stub-covered road ditch and crawled over to his kittens. "Ain't no one gonna take no chance on whether you live or not! Now git quiet!"

His clothes were wet from the weeds, but the air was still plenty warm. Hey, all that wetness was not him! "Coalie, you are a scoundrel, sure 'nough!" Coalie pushed his nose into the pile of kittens.

"Git out of here. Now come on, we got a long walk back home. Stay away from these kittens, y'hear?"

He thought it best to get off the road. Cutting across a hayfield with the kittens squirming in his arms, he hit Number One Ditch and walked across it on logs and little islands of dirt. Coalie waded across and came out on the other side wet and muddy.

Rass could easily find his way home if he followed the drainage ditches and kept the path straight across from ditch to ditch. He preferred walking along a ditch bank any day to the road. There were always a few sprigs of henpepper or sheepshire to munch on.

When he reached Four Ditch, no logs lay across it, so he waded. It felt good. The bottom was a little sandy and that made the wading good. It felt smooth. It also made him wonder if it might not be just as well to go north up Four Ditch and wade a while longer.

No, he'd better follow the sure way of keeping a straight line, because the very lives of the kittens depended on him. At least he could take a short rest and let his feet hang in the cool water. He nestled his toes in the soothing sand. The kittens romped about.

As the kittens ran up the ditch bank, Rass lay a restricting arm around Ole Coalie and watched a crawdad pile up a chimney of mud near the water's edge. It would be great to live like this all the time. The heads of two water snakes glided by and reminded him that he still had to face Dad when he got home. A baby bullfrog hopped right over his legs. The little striped kitten chased a dragonfly, and he called to it, "Better come back here. That old dragonfly is a witch doctor and could cast a spell on you."

Rass found he was laughing out loud, but it seemed sort of hollow to be laughing when no one else was there. Besides, it was getting a little bit dark. Guess he would not say any more about witch doctors because it sounded too much like the ghost stories Dad scared the little girls with. Not that he believed a word.

Any way you looked at it, it was not right for Dad to tell ghost stories. Now, what if one of the little girls were out alone late on a cloudy day like this? They would be plumb scared. Ole lady Pratts had to be sent to the asylum 'cause of strangeness.

Well, he wasn't lost and he wasn't scared. Fact was, he wasn't scared of ghost stories or nothing! He never got scared of anything that was not a sight-proven fact. Now it was perfectly all right to be afraid of a tornado if you saw it coming right before your eyes or a fire in a schoolhouse, but until you knew something for a fact it was just plain sissy to get scared.

The daylight was going fast now, but Rass could still see the black kitten as it went bounding out into the brush. He called, but the kitten kept running. Then, as he started after it he heard the squeaks of a dying field mouse. "Did you hear that, Coalie? I knowed that black one was a wild one. I declare he can look out for hisself." Rass turned back to check on the other two kittens.

He heard the black kitten getting farther and farther away, and then he heard it no longer. Dark sifted in so fast now, he was forced to think of himself and the other two kittens. He caught them and hurried toward Five Ditch. He would know that ditch even in the dark; he fished there regularly.

Walking along the end row of corn was the surest way to remain in a straight line, and then there would be a pasture fence that led right down to the ditch so the cows could water themselves. "Coalie, we're the same as home, boy! Now all we got to do is find a hidin' place for the kittens and figure up a good tale to tell why we been out so late. Here's the ditch! What happened to the pasture, Oh bother. Jist help me find that blame path!"

His hands and feet hit nothing but underbrush. Trees

grew almost down to the water's edge. There were no stars out, for it was still misting, but the water seemed to pick up a little light from somewhere. Something moved in the brush! Rass stood motionless, frozen still. Whatever it was, was not small from the sounds it was making. Maybe it was a mountain lion like in his Western book. No. That was a silly. Fact was, there were no mountain lions in these parts. He *had* to remember the facts! He wished for another person, any person.

Something was making those sounds! *Crunch, crack, crunch!* He clutched the kittens tighter. A little too tight. One of them bolted from his arms. But his call for it stuck in his throat, and he started to tremble from head to toe. It was very dark. He could stand and shout at the animal, or whatever it was, or maybe stay quiet and run. The lost kitten was probably safer where it had run to than he was. He took a few cautious steps. The sounds had stopped. He waited, but they did not start again.

Something brushed him from the other side. A bark and a nudge told him that it was Ole Coalie. Coalie pushed ahead as if he were certain where he was going. Gosh dang, it was dark enough to scare a grown man!

Coalie barked an invitation, and Rass decided to follow. He stubbed his foot and fell. This could not be Five Ditch, for there was no decent path. Maybe he had turned north instead of south! He stuck his hand into the water and checked to see which way it was running. He had turned right.

Something wiggled beneath him. It was his last kitten. He pulled it out from under him and cradled it in his hand as he sat up. He was crying and no one could hear him, and he was sad and glad for that. He cried, "Coalie, I'm lost. I want to git home!"

Coalie licked his face and then started across the ditch.

"Don't cross that ditch, Coalie. We'll git more lost if we do."

He heard another sound in the bush behind him. The thing was moving again! There was nothing left to do! In terror he waded into the ditch after Ole Coalie, feeling the way with his feet by habit and hoping not to come to a drop-off. He heard the thing splash into the water behind him.

Coalie was yelping and moving across an empty field now, and Rass followed, half running and falling in the darkness. The thing was so close behind him that he could have touched it. His teeth set tight with fear. Then the creature made a familiar sound. Rich old Mr. Pritse's mean breeding bull was after him! Angry hooves pounded the dirt and crunched through the stubs and dried grass.

Amidst the snorting, meowing, yelping, and his own shouting, Rass realized that he was no longer lost. That had been Six Ditch he had just crossed, not Five. He was in Pritse's pasture! He ran faster and kept one arm out to find the barbed-wire fence that he knew surrounded the pasture. He went on and on blindly, groping, stumbling over the rough field.

Coalie jumped against him, knocking him down. He clutched his kitten as he hit the ground, and rolled. Barbed wire tore his skin and his shirt. It did not matter; that same old barbed wire had stopped the bull!

He lay there panting and hugging the kitten in one arm. With his other tired, sore arm, he reached out to stroke Ole Coalie. "We're safe! We're safe, Ole Coalie dog! You're smarter than any story-book dog, I declare. Wish I could tell somebody what you jist done for me!"

He stood up to look for lights where he knew his house to be. There they were. Home! Home meant a licking, it meant fighting with Dad or L.G., but a light was on and he was afraid of nothing that he could see.

He heard the *hack, hack, hack* of someone chopping wood. As he got closer, he smelled the rotten smell of the pigs' soured milk. Enough light came through for him to see that the kitten he still held was Snowball. He smoothed the wet fur and said, "I can hide you easy in the hog-killin' barrel and lay that piece of woven wire over the top, but now you got to git quiet!"

It took a couple of seconds for him to realize that the meowing he was hearing was not coming from Snowball. Ole Coalie shot past him in pursuit of a screaming, fur-stiffened, little striped kitten. They ran right between the legs of Dad, who was standing by the wood pile holding a lantern high over his head so he could see.

"Rass, that you out there?" Dad called.

Rass ducked behind the pile of fragrant, freshly cut cookwood. This called for thinking he had not rehearsed, but he was scared of nothing now. "Yeah, I been fishin' Five Ditch, and I had to go out searchin' for that black scoundrel, Coalie. And to make matters worse he went and scared a couple of them kittens back home." At that he dropped Snowball and kicked him so he would start running too.

The rest of the family were at the door now, and they crowded around Rass, almost cutting off his air. The kittens were tearing around the wood and the little girls were trying to catch them.

Sally said, "Ain't it wonderful, Dad? You already killed 'em onct, and now they come back to life, like in a ghost story. It really goes to prove they do have nine lives, jist like you said, Dad!"

52

The girls took the kittens into the house and Dad did not stop them, and Rass knew Dad would not try to get rid of them after Sally had said it was like in a ghost story. Dad loved to scare the little girls with his ghost stories.

He snatched up a willow stick. "Come learn your lesson for stayin' out late, Rass."

Mom called to Rass as he followed Dad out behind the smokehouse. "When your lickin's over, git them muddy clothes off 'fore you come trackin' in the house, and put that shirt in cold water so's the blood don't set."

Later in bed, looking at the familiar slope of his ceiling and the cracks in the heavy brown wallpaper, Rass felt good. He had never really been afraid out there. Maybe a little nervous, but the fact remained that he had been among strangeness and had managed to come out of it all by himself. Almost for sure, the black kitten was still alive as well as the two that had come back with him. Just lying there, hearing Dad shouting at L.G. to get into bed, gave him a home feeling.

Four

Rass spent the rest of the summer fighting. Fighting off the bother of the little girls, who kept coming to him with their problems, because Mom was too busy to listen and Dad never listened to girl talk. Fighting because he was the one always stuck with being around the house to help out— Dad's orders. All the while L.G. showed off by joining the menfolk and even getting to help bale hay. That was reason enough for lots of the fights.

But Rass's longest continuing fight was with Grandpa. All year long, Grandpa demanded, raved, and kicked, and squirted tobacco juice. Well, it wasn't really a fight he had with Grandpa because he managed it so well, but it was necessary to let Grandpa believe it was fighting. He let Grandpa force him to listen to ways a body could make money off the land. In turn, he got to mention out loud some of his own ideas about planting rice and some of the other scientific things he'd been talking to Mr. Aaral about at school.

He hauled in new pots of dirt for Grandpa's land experiments when one got kicked over or started smelling too much. By egging on an argument, he always managed to keep Grandpa in high spirits. He let Sally take care of showing affection to Grandpa and let Dad pay for the oysters Grandpa craved. So all in all, Grandpa was not neglected.

By the fall of Rass's tenth year, he guessed he'd carried at least a hundred bowls of oyster stew from the big house to

Grandpa's little house. Mom never made a pot of it willingly.

"The very idea, Grandpa havin' to send off an' get canned oysters when we cain't afford 'em! Throws a big stink till he gits the thangs an' then eats 'em, guts an' all. I'll tell you, he ain't like regular folks!" Mom was irritatedly stirring the oyster stew and complained with a voice filled with contempt and aggravation. "Here it is, Rass. Take 'em to 'im an' git 'em out of my sight!"

Rass took the stewer by the handle and watched his step as he went out the back door and across the yard to Grandpa's little house. Dad bought oysters and tolerated Grandpa's railing only because he knew the old man could not live forever.

"Who is it? That you, Sally? Did you pick me some greens like I told y'to? I said, is that you, Sally?"

"No, Grandpa. It's me, Rass, I got your oyster stew."

"Stop bein' so poky and git in here with it!" Grandpa had the corners of his mouth drawn back into his beard and squirted a stream of tobacco juice right into Rass's path.

"Look, you want me to spill it, or do y'want me to watch my step an' git it to you?"

"Damn kid! Not a bit of respect for your elders! Set it down! Hmph! Needs pepper! Where's my pepper?" Grandpa could reach almost everything in the small room from his old rocking chair, and he was as set in his ways as Dad.

"I'd pepper it *good,* Grandpa! It covers up the sight of the guts!"

"Hogwarsh, you're talkin'! What do you know about seafood! Y'ain't been ten miles from home! You need to travel, like Willis, and git a little learnin' in you, boy! You been around your mother too long!" Grandpa wiped stew drippings off his beard and moustache with a towel napkin. He was the only person in the family that used napkins.

"Tell me about Boston, Grandpa."

"Boston . . . Boston. In Boston, boy, I could buy a bucket of oysters this big for five cents in the old days! You ain't tasted a real oyster 'til you've had it on the half shell!"

"I ain't tasted a oyster at all and I'm not aimin' to!"

When he said that, Grandpa sputtered out a mouthful of stew, and Rass helped him wipe it up. He listened to him rave on about oysters and Boston until the stew was all gone, then handed him his molasses, which he always had for dessert, and took the stewer back to Mom.

"Well, how'd you make out? I see he et it all," Mom said.

"Boy, Grandpa sure likes to rant, so I jist give him somethin' to rant about an' stand back," said Rass.

Sally said, "Grandpa said I could have his trunk and all the pictures and the I.O.U.'s and everything in it when he dies!"

"Huh!" said Mom. "With his disposition, he'll live to be a hundred and three, jist like his sister did! He ain't dead yet by a walloping! Dad might do better settin' him straight now 'bout family ways 'stead holdin' out for him to die 'fore long."

"Mom, Preacher Hoyt says you're s'posed to love one another. You sure don't love Grandpa!" Sally said.

"Well, it's not him I hate. I jist hate the ways he's got about him," Mom answered.

"I got to git on back to the cotton patch. It's already past one. Dad 'lowed that me and L.G. better git that patch picked clean by the end of the day." Rass left Mom and Sally still talking and joined L.G. in the hot sun of the cotton field. They worked hard. Rass had about forgotten what it meant to rest, and Dad said to get his mind off the word. Near sundown L.G. made him a proposition.

"You pick the last two rows and I'll do the barn chores. Is it a deal?"

Rass had nothing to lose. "Okay; it's a deal." He listened while a bobwhite whistled and then went back to picking while the cows mooed and booed and fussed.

He had picked about halfway through the first row when he saw L.G. coming back to the field. "What's the big idea? We made a deal. Y'cain't back out now!" he called.

"Grandpa's dead!" said L.G.

Rass stood still, staring, waiting for the words to disappear like the moon behind a cloud. "No, he ain't! You're a lar!" He started to cry and swung at L.G. "You're a lar!"

L.G. was not lying. No one lied with such a mournful and shocked look on his face. It was true. Grandpa was dead. Rass dropped his bag of cotton there in center field and started walking back to the house with L.G.

"Who found him?"

"Mom. She fixed up the rest of that can of oysters for his supper and when she took it out to the little house he wasn't yellin' or nothin'. She pushed his door open, and there he sat in his rocker, jist starin' out into space."

"Does Sally know?"

"Yeah, she knows. She's bawlin' somethin' dreadful out behind the smokehouse."

"Y'ain't supposed to cry at death, but she's a girl, so I guess it's all right. Did you see him?"

"Mom won't let no one go in the little house. I'm not wontin' to anyway," said L.G.

"Old age killed him. It's bound to've been old age. Everybody's got to die, if for no other cause than old age," Rass reasoned out loud.

"Here comes Sally and she's still bawlin'. Gad's sake, I wish she'd stop bawlin'," L.G. said.

"Grandpa's dead, Rass," Sally told him.

"Sally, y'knew he had to die. Y'knew he was gettin' childish and ornery. Y'knew he'd have to die purtty soon," Rass said.

Sally reached out for his hand and he jerked away. "What you cryin' for? Y'knew he was goin' to die, Dad's been saying it right along." Rass was not going to let his feelings go. Didn't Sally know he was a boy and could not?

"I cain't help it! Oh, Rass, Grandpa saw Abraham Lincoln! He cut wood for the war widders in the Civil War, and he let lots of people barry his money. He was a good man! Why did God let him die?"

"God cain't let people go on livin' forever, else we'd be piled up one on top of the other on this earth. And Grandpa was ornery. He yelled at Mom all the time, and he tripped Sissy with his cane."

Sally cried, "Stop it. Y'cain't talk about the dead like that!"

"Well, I ain't making' up no lies about him bein' sugary sweet. He never claimed to be."

L.G. agreed. "He'd argue with you till he was black in the face if he thought for a minute y'was tryin' to make him out to be Santa Claus."

"He never did yell at me," Sally sobbed.

"Reckon he never, Sally," L.G. said softly to her. "You was his pet." He could not take any more of Sally's tears. "I got to git at the barn chores," he said, and quickly ran ahead. A rabbit was scared out of hiding. It ran a distance, stopped to listen, and then ran on. Rass glanced toward the house. There was already a car in the front yard and Dad was talking to a man. Guess he might as well walk on a little closer and see who was there. It was Uncle Jake.

Then Rass's feet moved in the direction of the little house. His hands mechanically opened the door. There sat Grandpa, a bit of molasses still clinging to his moustache above his opened mouth. His eyes were staring, just like L.G. had said. Wonder if Dad would get a camera to take a picture of them, to see what he was looking like at the last. Guess not. People only did that in case of murder, and Grandpa died of old age. Gads, it was quiet. It was terribly quiet.

If only Grandpa would spit some tobacco juice or swing his cane at him. It was not right to see a human sitting with absolutely no movement. Wonder if he's still got feelings? Rass thought. He pushed Grandpa a little with his hand. Wonder where the mind goes when you die? Everybody has to die. Preacher Hoyt says it. Mom and Dad say it. People have died for thousands of years. If you don't get killed, you got to die of old age.

Wonder how Grandpa will feel when they throw all that dirt on him? Rass thought then. Must be dreadful to be buried. He had got buried in the hayloft once for just a minute, and he never wanted that to happen again. But you had to bury dead people. And Grandpa was dead.

Rass felt pain shoot through his hand and realized he had been hitting the door with all his might. He looked up to see Dad standing there.

"Go crank up Jake's car, Rass, an' wipe your eyes. It ain't fittin' for men and boys to cry," Dad said.

"He died like you said he would! Guess you won't have to buy no more oysters. You're glad, ain't you? Where y'takin' him?" he shouted at Dad.

"Durbin. He'll be buried beside Grandma after all these thirty years. He never did hanker to marry anyone else." Dad's shoulders curved even more than usual.

"Is there any such place as hell, Dad?"

"Ain't no use askin' questions like that."

"Grandpa tole me there wasn't."

"He believed like he wanted to, I guess. In a way, we all do."

"He said God woulda been plumb foolish to make all us people so's he could burn us up later."

"Ain't gonna profit you none, nor change thangs a whit to question and talk about it. Help me along with the crankin' now."

Dad had not really cared for Grandpa, Rass thought. Why did he have to frown and talk hateful when Grandpa had just died? Why couldn't Dad like his own father? Rass decided not to ever marry and have children. So that would put an end to that.

He cranked the car and left it running and walked out toward the open field. He looked at the great round red sun as it set. One of the kittens skittered in front of him. A breeze twisted the cotton stalks. Everybody's got to die! His stomach turned. He grabbed it, doubling over. He was going to vomit.

Things became silent. The car motor had stopped. Dad was shouting, "Rass, get back here! L.G., hitch up the horses. Don't argue with me, Jake! When Pa leaves this place, he's goin' in my car. Git a move on, boys, we're goin' to town. Jake, you'll do well to leave. When Pa leaves my place, it'll be in *my* car!"

They went to town and Dad took out a loan and picked out a car the same day. Grandpa *was* going to go to Durbin in Dad's car.

Five

Things went back to normal, with work and more work, but there were still moments for Rass to talk to his kittens and to dream of being out doing great things with Willis on the ranch. He and the other boys finished picking the cotton. Even the bolls had been pulled and ginned now. Coolness had come in to change the lush green fields to brown stubble. Christmas was practically here, and Dad had threatened him with severe punishment if he told the little girls that there was no such thing as Santa Claus.

Rass had had no intention of telling the little girls, but Sally was eight. He sure hadn't believed in Santa Claus when he was eight.

He guessed Sally was just as stupid as he had always thought she was. Sally believed that, after she had picked the doll or whatever it was she wanted most out of Sears's Christmas catalog, Santa would bring it, providing it did not cost too much. Now how dumb could a girl get? He liked Christmas as well as anyone, but he knew good and well that the presents got ordered and stashed away in the smokehouse until Christmas night, when Dad and Mom made a big to-do with their pretending and brought them into the house.

"L.G., do you think Dad would go ahead and git us them roller skates we want even if it is winter?" he asked.

that he had had to throw her doll over the banister. If Dad had let him lay into Sally, like she had it coming, there would have been no cause to. But no, Sally was a girl, and he was not allowed to fight girls.

Rass got up and walked away. He did not know why he had let himself start to get soft-hearted anyway. He ought to have layed into Roselee, too, with her trying to claim Snowball for her own and half drowning him trying to baptize him. It had taken him two hours getting Snowball back to normal. He ought to be rough with the girls, and that would show them all, including Dad!

He went into the dining room and told Roselee and Sissy to get out. They were chasing each other around the table again. They knew that that was the way he had got his nose broken. Sally came in and set nine big bowls around the table and one little one for Mary. If Willis and Rass's oldest sister, Bertie, who was married, still lived at home, they would really have a table full. It would sure be nice if Willis could make it home for Christmas. In his last letter Willis had said he might not be able to swing it.

Bertie and her husband, Verge, who always brought along chewing gum, would be over Christmas night. Sally said she sure missed Bertie. Maybe Bertie was to Sally the way Willis was to him. But there he was, getting soft again. Mom said Christmas softened up most people. Bertie was soft all the time, and she used nice-sounding words that could touch a body the same as a hand could, and she smelled all sweet and flowery and unnatural. Mom smelled natural, like bacon fat and lye soap and garden greens, but if he had to pick a woman, he guessed he would pick Bertie's kind.

Well, he'd better go out and carry in a load of wood and get soft thoughts like that out of his head. The good peppery smell of chili teased him as he walked through the kitchen.

"L.G., come on and let's git this wood in. I can see Dad comin'. Keep quiet about my spat with Sally."

He got loaded up and reached the back door just as Dad and the older boys went in. He stuck his foot out to hold the door open until he could work the big armload of wood through.

"Keep that door closed, Rass. We're not heatin' up the whole outdoors. People would think you were born in a barn," Dad said.

"Nope, I was born in the wide-open spaces in the middle of a tornado."

Mom said, "Honor your parents, Rass, or face your Maker."

"Oh, Rass," Sally whispered, "don't sass like that. Santa will hear you!"

Dad cracked him one with the towel. "Don't sass me again!" Then Dad turned to Mom and asked, "Havin' chili? Thought you was savin' that in case Willis got to come home Christmas."

"I had two blocks of chili, not one. Christmas ain't but two days away. I reckon I can keep the other block two days. I ain't done too bad managin' groceries all these years you've been married to me," Mom said.

Dad said, "I ain't complainin'. You've been a good help to me. You've seen us through some mighty slim times, especially these last two years. Not a one of us has had to leave the table hungry."

Gosh, dang, Christmas was softening up Dad! It even had *him* paying compliments.

Mom turned back the oilcloth and placed the chili pot on the bare boards of the table. Everyone found his place and Dad reached for a biscuit.

"It takes a good cook to make biscuits like these," Dad said.

Mom sure *ought* to make good biscuits—she made between

eighty and a hundred every day! Eighty if they had corn bread for supper and a hundred if they had biscuits for supper. Ole Coalie got the left-over ones unless someone wanted a butter sandwich between meals. Rass stuck a nice warm one in his pocket to give Coalie after supper.

"These girls been mindin' you? Santa's been watchin'," Dad said.

The little girls started talking all at once about what they wanted Santa to bring. Sally said, "I want a doll with long hair."

"Not a big girl like you? Santa might think you're gettin' a little big for a doll," Dad said.

"I'll say she is!" Rass couldn't help blurting out.

"Rass, no one asked for your opinion. Better let what you got to eat stop your mouth!" Dad snapped. Then he looked back toward Sally and said, "I'll bet Santa has had his eyes on them purtty pictures your teacher bragged about at school. Maybe he would like to see you do more of 'em. Santa likes it when you mind your teacher."

Oh, so that was the story. Dad wasn't getting Sally a doll. Rass wondered about his roller skates. A body could see right through Dad's persuasion, but it never stopped him none. Guess Dad didn't care if Sally got disappointed. Was that being nice to girls?

"Santa might like you to draw him a nice picture and leave it for him alongside of the pigtail," Dad said.

"Oh, lands, I better not forget to put that pigtail in the bean pot Christmas Eve. Wouldn't do to make Santa mad," Mom said in a voice awkward at pretending.

Mom never had forgotten the pigtail; Dad wouldn't let her. Ecck! It made Rass sick just to think about eating one! He picked up his bowl of chili and headed for the living room.

"I'm gonna set by the heatin' stove. Santa ain't got his eyes on me."

Poor Sally looked at him in disbelief as he walked past her. He knew he was worrying her with his words.

The next day Rass came charging home from school angry as a cotton-gin owner forced to stop the machinery because of a bonnet caught in the chute. "Them Cross twins come down with the mumps, and now Miz Noelte thinks she's goin' to git me and L.G. to run around on the stage tonight in our underwear with a bunch of paper stuck on us playin' like we're snowflakes. Well, I ain't goin' to do no sich thang, and she can put that in her craw and chew it!"

"Rass, give Mom that paper. It's got my directions on it too," Sally said, and grabbed the paper from him. "I'm goin' to be a walkin', talkin' doll with curly hair. It says you got to curl my hair, Mom!"

Mom read the paper and wrinkled her brow. "This is carryin' thangs a little too far. I'll use the curlin' iron on you, Sally, but your dad wouldn't think of lettin' you out in knee-socks and short panties. When a teacher starts dictatin' that much, I'd say she's gone a little too far!"

Maybe Mom was on Rass's side, too. "I'll say!" he agreed. "When a teacher starts dictatin' that you have to be in a fool play, she's gone a little too far. I ain't takin' no dictatin'!"

Rass did not even bother to take his coat off, but walked back outside. He could do his barn chores and then maybe fool around with Ole Coalie and the cats until after they all had left for the Christmas party at school. He had always liked going before. Just everybody in the whole country went, but he would not go tonight and get stuck in any old play.

He stayed there quite a while until Dad came, calling, "Rass, find the car crank. I've tole you a hundred times to keep your hands off'n my car tools, and that includes the crank. Now cough it up! You're goin to cause us all to be late."

He went to the car shed. Mom claimed Dad had bought the car because of Uncle Jake, but Dad claimed it was to protect the little ones from the weather. He found the crank lying on the fender just where Dad had laid it after he got through showing off the car to Mr. Brown yesterday. Dad cranked the car up and backed it out and sat there steaming in the cold night air waiting for the rest of the family. Rass stood in the shed watching.

Sally came out in a red crepe-paper dress, her hair an explosion of kinky red-blond curls and half her legs showing naked.

Dad yelled, "What in the thunderation? Git that kid back in the house and put some clothes on her!"

"That's the way the teacher said she had to be," said Mom.

"She'll die of pneumonia in weather like this. No sense in me goin' deeper in debt for a car and then have her run out in winter half naked," Dad said.

Mom went in the house and came back with a blanket and threw it around Sally and pushed her into the car. Everyone else piled in, and Dad switched on the headlights. That was the end of Rass's hiding place. "Git in the car, Rass!" Dad shouted.

"No teacher is goin' to dictate me into no play!" he said.

"You'll mind your teacher and do as she says, and I'm tellin' you right now to git in this car!"

No use expecting Dad to care about his feelings, not even if he lived to be as old as Grandpa did. He crawled in and sat on Frank's lap. A person could hardly breathe when the whole family was in the car at one time.

When they arrived he figured he would just sit out in the car, but a scream from Sally made him look up. Willis was standing there, smiling, in the center of the lighted schoolhouse door! He had swung it, after all. My, he looked bigger than Dad by far with that heavy overcoat, and his hair looked yellower than ever under his white snow-covered cap. Oh, boy! Willis was home!

Rass told Willis his problem, and right away Willis talked to Mrs. Noelte. That night Rass and L.G. sat on either side of Willis and watched the play from the audience. When Mrs. Noelte knew for sure that Rass would not be in the play she had let L.G. go too. She said it would not give the right effect to have just one snowflake. Instead, at the time when they were to have done that stupid dance, she reached her arm out on stage and tossed some cut-up paper into the air. Now why hadn't she thought of that in the first place and saved all the ruckus?

The next night at exactly eight thirty, Dad gave the bed-time order; it made no difference that it was Christmas Eve. As usual, Rass's cat, Snowball, ran for the stairs to race him to bed, but this time, which was quite unusual, one of L.G.'s cats followed.

"Git them cats outta the house!" Dad demanded.

"It's Christmas Eve, and old Tom wanted to come in too," L.G. pleaded.

Dad said, "I don't want any cats in the house tonight. This place has got to be quiet, or Santa won't come."

Mom said, "They'll settle down. It *is* Christmas."

"I'd better not catch 'em in here tomorrow night!" Dad

warned, and he picked up little Mary, who had fallen asleep behind the heating stove, and carried her into the little girls' room just off the living room. Dad sure was softening up again.

Dad came back into the living room just in time to settle the argument about whether the size of the sock determined how much candy a person got.

"Now Santa ain't gonna cheat nobody, you can bank on that, so git things fixed and git in bed. Santa don't come to no one unless they're sound asleep," Dad said.

Dad knew how to *talk* equal, but there was no point in taking chances. It would be just natural for him to put in extras in the girls' longer stockings. Rass got a paper bag and set it under his sock for extras, and L.G. did the same. Willis stood there and laughed at them.

They went up to their beds, and Rass lay there talking to Willis until Dad threatened them again to quiet down. He lay there in the dark for a long while wondering if he would get the roller skates. He was almost dead sure that it was skates he'd seen in the pile of things in the smokehouse.

How much longer would he have to wait to know for sure if the little girls were asleep? After that, Rass planned to ask Dad if he could help fill the stockings. Willis had done it once. He had told him so. Rass was going to turn eleven in a couple of months, and he ought to be big enough to help. He kept waiting and waiting, but Sally was so worried about that doll he did not think she would get to sleep very fast.

The next thing Rass was aware of was a screeching, hissing noise coming from the little girls' room. He must have dozed off. Gads! That was a cat fight, sure as Christmas comes on the twenty-fifth! He raced down the stairs and dashed into the room just ahead of Dad. Dad whispered roughly, "Rass, what you doin' up? Never mind, jist git them cats outta there! I told you to keep them out tonight, didn't I?"

Rass crawled under the girls' bed and pulled the cats out. He could not do a thing to stop the noise; he would be clawed to pieces if he tried. He held on to Snowball and handed Dad Old Tom. He closed the door to the girls' room and said out loud, "L.G. had no business lettin' his barn cat come in."

"No cat has any business in the house Christmas night. Now git 'em back outside and keep the door shut like you've been told. If you'd done it in the first place, this wouldn't have happened. And keep your voice down," Dad said, raising his own voice all the while.

"Let me help fill the stockin's; Willis told me he helped once."

Dad never said a word but reached for the razor strop.

Mom said, "Ain't no kids helpin' fill stockin's. You'll wait till mornin' to fiind out what's in your'n, like the rest. Shut up now or you'll have them girls awake for sure!"

Rass put the cats outside and locked the door securely and went back upstairs. It was pure luck, or Dad's being Christmas-soft, that he got by without a licking. He worked his way under the heavy covers. The floor sure made a person's feet cold. Well, he guessed he'd wait until next year to help fill the stockings like Willis.

He had not had time to settle back into sleep when he heard someone yell, "Merry Christmas!" It sounded something like Uncle Tut's voice, but not exactly either.

"Git in out of the cold." Dad's voice was urgent with forced quietness.

Dad would really give it to Rass if he caught him out of bed again, but his curiosity was swelling up to the investigating point. He crept down the stairs and pressed his eye hard against the crack in the knotty sawmill-marked pine-board door that led to the living room. Uncle Tut was there with his legs buckling and bowing, and he was throwing his chest out, proclaiming the way to spend a perfect Christmas.

"Thought ya might like some banazas or coconuts," slurred Uncle Tut.

Dad said, "I ain't one to give advice by nature, but by gum, Tut, you'd better take them thangs home to your own kids. It's gittin' late and Prudy will be waitin' for you."

"Ah bets ya don' hav' any banazas or coconuts."

"We got plenty. I never disappointed my kids on a Christmas yet, which is more than I can say for you!"

"Oh, bless you. Bet ya never giv' a bottle to our dear ole Pa when he was alive."

Dad's face looked strange—sober, but vicious. "You better git movin'."

"Now tha'z a fine way to trea' company." Uncle Tut cast the words at Dad as he stumbled through the front door, causing a coconut to go rolling across the front porch. "I'm goin' to Jake's. Now there's good lovin' brother."

"Drunker'n a chicken with a 'rung neck!" Dad said after Uncle Tut was gone.

"On Christmas night, too. Lord have mercy. And him claimin' to be a preacher!" Mom said.

At least Uncle Tut loved everybody when he was drunk. Dad never got drunk. Rass wondered if Dad would be nice to him if he ever should, just by accident, drink some whiskey and get drunk?

He did not want to hear any more. He went silently back up the stairs and finally fell asleep.

Dad's roaring "Git up!" was the music that woke him. He and L.G. pushed and shoved until they both landed in a heap at the bottom of the stairs. Mom stood guard by the living room while Dad took the little girls out to the front porch to see if they could hear the last sounds of the sleigh bells as Santa drove away. Sally was standing next to Rass, and he tried to push her out with Mary and Sissy and Rose-lee, but she would not budge.

"What's the matter with you, Sally? Go on!"

"No, Rass. There ain't no use. I know there ain't no Santa Claus." There were big tears in her eyes. Of all the luck! She was going to mess up the perfect moment when they all got their presents.

"Oh, there is too, Sally. Go on." He pushed her again.

"Don't push me, Rass. I heard you with the cats last night. And I saw you peekin' when Uncle Tut come, too. Oh Rass, a preacher like Uncle Tut!" She had the saddest crumpled face he had ever seen in his whole life. The depth of hopelessness that came through her voice made him reach into his pocket and get his lucky rabbit foot and give it to her. It was getting worn out, but it still ought to help her some. And here he was being nice to Sally in spite of his determination not to be!

"Sally, we're goin' to git to see our presents now, and if you don't act happy I'll twist your arm!"

Everyone crowded through the door at one time, like chickens under a brooder stove. Rass wanted something awful to look toward his own stocking but would not let himself do it until he saw whether Sally had got her doll. She had a great big paint set and a wrapped-up package. He saw her slowly open it, and then her eyes burst into a glow as she held up a doll with long hair.

"From Willis! Oh, Rass, we don't need Santa, we got Willis!"

That was enough. Rass grabbed for his sock and the paper

bag with roller skates sticking out of the top. He started buckling them on when he realized he had a wrapped-up package too. Now what in the world would Willis be giving him?

It was a genuine hand-braided bullwhip! Man, oh, man! Then he realized he was wiping tears from his own eyes. Christmas sure could soften a person up.

Six

For quite a time the feeling of Christmas continued to hang over the house. Rass made good use of his Christmas presents for two months, but he did not depend on presents for most of his fun, the way some of the town kids did. He knew that some of them even got presents on their birthdays. He had a birthday coming up, but he was not in the least concerned about any old present. Just getting to be a year older was present enough. He would be eleven tomorrow and he could feel it already.

Racing with L.G. down the road ditch and outsmarting the ice fit his mood just fine. If he ran at just the right speed, he could go all the way to school on thin ice. With each step the ice broke behind him.

Sally walked straight and mighty in the middle of the road, holding her head high as if she were a lady of dignity. Maybe she thought she looked pretty in that green coat with a missing button and the large plaid parka that had trouble hiding her straggling hair, but her long, wrinkled underwear made her look tacky. Let her freeze. Girls were too stupid to wear pants! And every time she shook her finger her coat flew open, only to be clutched shut again.

Rass had let Sally carry the reading book that they shared at school now that he'd got stuck in Miss Noelte's fourth- and fifth-grade room with her. It was enough to hang on to his lunch bucket.

Crack! Crack! Crack! went his steps, and the time allowed before a foot would go all the way through was getting narrower. Oops! His foot went partly under that time.

"If you boys don't git back on the road, you'll git a wet foot for sure, and y'll freeze all day," Sally said.

"I ain't got a wet foot yet," answered L.G.

"Sally, jist go on to school and keep quiet. You're too big of a baby to have a little fun," said Rass.

"I'm almost as old as you! Jist one year!" Sally answered smartly.

Rass almost lost his timing. "You are two years younger!"

"Ha! Last Monday I turned nine, and you're still ten, so you're jist one year older now!"

"A birthday don't make y'gain a year," put in L.G.

"It certainly does! Oh! Look at you, Rass. Your shoe is wet. You won't ever listen to reason. I'm goin' to tell," Sally said.

He kept right on running on the ice for a little way, and then he came out to the center of the crisp-frozen mud of the dirt road and kicked his wet shoe and said, "Try to prove it. My foot will be dry by night. I'll tell them you're lyin'."

Sally pursed her lips. "Dad could easily tell if a shoe had been soaked It ruins the leather."

"That's all you know about boys' shoes! High tops can stand a lot. You think like a girl!" Rass leaped back into the road ditch and began running on the ice again.

"You cain't think at all! I'm not goin' to talk to you anymore." Sally threw back her head with a jerk of finality.

"Good!" He turned to yell back to her, and his shoe went all the way through the ice. "Is that a promise? No use talkin' to you. You're a girl, and stupid besides!" he added.

"Good-bye," Sally said. She cut off from the dirt road and climbed the barbed-wire fence.

She was going to walk through the field to the gravel road to try for a ride in Hickman's truck and beat Rass and L.G. to school. So what? They were in no hurry. What could a teacher do but put a check on her book if you were late? On second thought, maybe Rass would cut across the field too and hitch a ride on the tailgate of the truck. That was always a good feeling, with the wind whistling and the motor roaring and a body holding on with just one hand.

The mud in the fields was frozen enough to make easy walking. Rass made his steps fit the spacing of the fallen cornstalks. The *crunch, crunch, crunch* of the frozen stalks made rhythmic sounds as his weight crushed them, and seemed to say, "Eleven years old, eleven years old." Eleven was old enough to do as you pleased.

Rass brushed out the sound of L.G. yelling for him to come back to the road ditch. Under the pignut tree would be a good place to sit and watch for the big Hickman men to come out and put spoiled little Pam in the truck cab. She was an only child in the family.

He fixed the barbed wire so that two strands hooked together. It would be easy to scoot under in a hurry. Then he sat down on the tree root and tried to crack one of the tiny tough-shelled pecans that he called pignuts. It was getting colder; he could feel it penetrate his pants. Better sit on the lunch bucket; one more dent in the top would not matter. Rass reached around the tree for a larger rock to crack the pignut and stopped short. There sat Sally on her reader with her lunch bucket open, eating a Rex Jelly sandwich. Mom got all their lunch buckets by buying the half-gallon size of Rex Jelly.

"What are you doin' here?" he asked.

Sally looked at him with surprise and perplexity, stuffed the rest of the sandwich into her mouth, and muttered something as she closed her lunch bucket and ran. The Hickmans were loading! Rass grabbed his lunch bucket and ran too.

It sure was fine riding on the tailgate—a little colder than he had expected, but he was a boy and could stand lots of cold. Girls felt the cold easier, and two and a half miles was a long way for girls to walk to school in bad weather. If it stayed this cold, Mr. Pritse would offer his sisters a ride home for sure, as he had done every real bad day. Rass would *never* ride with Mr. Pritse, cold or not!

Oh, it was bound to be nice and warm in Mr. Pritse's car. Even in the summertime the windows were kept rolled up. Once he was not even allowed to roll a window down to let out a smell that he could not help. It was embarrassing. That sort of thing always happened when you were in school or at the table or someplace like Mr. Pritse's car, where it was not proper.

No one had said a word about it, thank goodness for that, but when they got out to walk the rest of the way home, Mr. Pritse had requested that Dad come see him at the gin the next day. It had cost Rass a sound licking and Dad the expense of a bottle of Listerine, because Mr. Pritse thought it was bad breath. Hanging on a tailgate was better, any way you cared to look at it.

Snow fell heavily all morning. With the ground already frozen, this snow might be a lasting one. Snow was fun, but it often melted too fast. However, by noon all the schoolchildren were pelting anyone within range with snowballs. After school it was the same thing. Rass rolled up a good one, with a rock forming the core. It really had power as it sailed . . . right into Mr. Sanders, the school principal!

Mr. Sanders marched him into the classroom and only let him out long enough to give L.G. a message.

"But don't tell Dad why I'm staying after, or I'll lay for you the minute I git home," Rass told him.

"Save your threats. I ain't tellin'," said L.G.

Rass had to stay after for so long that it was getting dark by the time he got to the railroad tracks—not that he minded. The cold had increased too. He had got over the first raw, cold feeling, and now things were going slow and easy. His feet moved onto the railroad ties methodically. He guessed he would not bother trying to walk the rails in this weather. He did not feel very peppy. The snow kept falling in little sleet needles and pecked at his face, but it all seemed nice and restful.

Dad strode into view out of the curtain of snow. "Rass! Rass, y'all right?"

"Yeah. Mr. Sanders didn't do nothin' but keep me after. It was his own fault for walkin' in front of a snowball and he knowed it, so I didn't git no lickin'."

Dad grabbed him by the hand and practically pulled him the rest of the way home. Dad sounded aggravated as he said, "You have a good enough sheep-lined coat. Why didn't you wear it? You're thankin' more like a two-year-old than eleven. Takin' off in weather like this in nothin' but an overall jumper! The temperature has already hit nineteen below and still droppin'!"

Dad scooped up a handful of snow and shoved him in through the back porch door and then started slapping snow all over his face. The other children all came running out. Rass didn't know what was happening.

Dad said, "Mom, you rub the wrist. I thank his face is gonna be okay." It was a strange feeling as Dad's hard knuckles scrubbed the snow across his cheek. Dad had never touched him before that he could remember, except to give him a licking. It was special to be touched. Sure was.

Mom said, "Now you kids clear out. We'll manage Rass all right. He ain't froze bad. Git back to your snowcream, 'fore it all melts."

Rass's face was starting to burn and sting. "Stop scratchin' me with that sleet. What y'mean, puttin' more snow on me if I'm froze? I'm getting my share of that snowcream!" He jerked away, hardly admitting to himself that Dad's touching him in kindness was as exciting as the thought of snowcream. Someday, when he got famous or something, then Dad would slap him on the back and say, "That's my son Rass!"

Dad jerked him right back. "If you go in by the fyar y'll git a bad sore!"

"Okay, so I won't set by the stove, but I'm aimin' to git some snowcream! I ain't had any for a whole year!" It was great to get so much attention.

Mom said, "Rass, the Lord means you to honor your father and obey, but Dad, I 'spect it'd be all right if he set at the end of the bed over by the door. There's still plenty of cold comin' in 'round that doorjamb." Mom practiced the old adage of "The hair of the dog kills the bite." She'd made him hold his finger close to the heating stove after he had burned it so it would heal faster, too.

When he walked into the living room the other children kept asking him, between mouthfuls of snowcream, about how it felt to be frozen. He pulled the reed-bottom kitchen chair to the foot of the bed and reared back in it until it balanced on the two back legs, gave audience to his admirers, and waited sedately for Mom to dish out his snowcream.

Mom talked as she dipped snowcream with a broken-handled teacup from the big white dishpan. "The snow came deep and clean the first couple hours. We had plenty of eggs and top cream on hand. I told little Mary, 'Jist no point in wastin' a *fine* chance for snowcream'. . . ." Mom talked a stream when things were going good, and she let people know her part in the goodness.

Rass's face hurt a bit, and his wrists were still stinging, but he felt fine inside and this feeling was accentuated by each mouthful of the sweet, fragrant vanilla snowcream.

After eating they gathered around Grandpa's big, fancy library table to do homework, and Sally said, "I cain't find my reader. What did y'do with it, Rass? You had it last!"

"Like heck I did! I ain't seen it all day!"

"It'll be in your desk in the morning, wait and see," Sally said, and then added, "I wish you really was two years older'n me and was in anuther grade."

"Sally, for the last time, I am two years older'n you! It won't hurt you to skip readin' practice onct. I never practice."

"You don't have to brag about it. People *know* y'don't jist by listenin' to you!" snapped Sally.

Mom said, "Shut the bickerin' and come eat. I'm jist havin' cornbread and milk enough to finish fillin' you up." But in the middle of the table sat a cake on the beautiful stand that had survived the tornado which had come through at the time Rass was born. It was a yellow cake with jam in the middle, like Mom always made for Sunday. Today was not Sunday, so Rass knew that it must be his birthday cake.

As they began to eat, Dad said, "Well, looks like Sally's catching up with you, Rass. She gained one year on you, and before you know it she'll gain that other year and you'll both be the same age!"

"See what I told you." Sally shook her finger at him. "Even Dad agrees with me."

"For cat's sake, Dad, why won't you tell Sally she really don't git a year closer to me jist cause she had a birthday?" he asked.

Dad reached for another piece of cornbread and crumbled it into his glass of milk and said, "Sure she does. Now dry up while Sally cuts this cake here." Dad plainly loved to side against him.

"That ain't *her* cake! It's mine! Ain't it, Mom? Sally had hern last week!"

Mom said, "Rass's birthday ain't till tomorrow, but I thought it'd warm him up a bit to have it tonight. Bein' froze ain't somethin' to take light." She handed him a sharpened, black-handled case knife.

He cut the cake in the middle and then quickly cut six pieces on either side. He put a piece on his own plate and started to eat it. It felt dry, and the seeds in the jam stuck between his teeth. No one knew that he didn't like cake and he wasn't telling. Cake was a treat, and he wanted his share!

As he got up from the table, Dad whacked him across the pants and the others eagerly joined in. "And one to grow on!" L.G. yelled, and really let him have it.

"Come outside, L.G., and try that again!" He tried to sound mad but couldn't. Anyway, he would like to see if he could lick L.G. now that he was eleven.

"You stay in the house, Rass! Hear me?" Mom scolded.

He raced L.G. upstairs to bed.

The next morning, the morning of his real birthday, he opened his eyes to see a shivering, goose-pimpled L.G. frantically clutching his clothes and trying to cover up and dress at the same time. The heaviness of the denim patch quilts kept him snuggled down in their warmth. This was one heck of a cold February. Eleven or not, he grabbed his pants and dashed across the chilly floor and downstairs to the King Heater.

"Rass, you're gettin' old enough to dress in your own room," Dad said right off.

"You want me to freeze again?"

"You ain't about to freeze inside a house. Grow up! Git yourself covered."

"I am covered. I got long underwear."

"Don't sass." Dad raised his hand as if to strike. Rass knew what that meant, so he returned to his bedside and quickly pulled on his pants and shirt, then carried his shoes and socks back down beside the all-engulfing warmth of the stove. That was safe enough. Everyone brought his shoes and socks to the stove to put them on, and everyone held to his own spot near the stove, too, because just a few feet away it was still cold in the room.

"I thank it's too cold to eat in the dinin' room," said Rass.

"Jist where do y'plan to have us eat? All settin' round the heatin' stove?" Mom asked. No trace of softness remained in her voice now. What did he have to do, go out and get frozen every day to make her speak nicer to him?

"Well, we do when we eat popcorn," he said.

"You're lettin' bein' eleven go to your head! Now stop your bossin' and git your chores done. I'm puttin' in the biscuits now."

Dad came in with another big log for the heater. "Keep the little girls home today. It's awful bad cold out. No use askin' for doctor bills. Rass, you can walk along with me soon

85

as I finish the chores in the barn. You'll be a little late, but it won't matter. I got to go buy a part for my shotgun. Won't hurt all you boys to dress extra warm. This is colder'n any February I can remember."

Rass waited and walked with Dad. He wore his old sheep-skin-lined jacket with the collar turned up around his neck and ears, and Dad had on his woolen overshirt. Rass felt sort of awkward walking with Dad. He wanted to say something, but couldn't think of anything to talk about. He never had just plain-talked with Dad. He ran a few feet ahead and broke the silence by singing eight verses of "Crawdad Hole."

"Don't thank you'll ever amount to much as a singer," Dad said.

"Never said I planned to be a singer."

"It's too cold to waste your breath sassin'."

Rass did not try to continue the conversation for the next half mile. Plain-talking took a lot of thought. Then he asked, "You a Republican or Democrat?"

"Now, Rass, you know blame well I'm Democrat, same as all the folks round here. Now stop askin' fool questions!"

"Not Grandpa! He wasn't Democrat! *He* was a Republi-can, an' he used to say all the Democrats have faces where their backside is!"

"Grandpa jist liked to argue! He'd argue a sign was black when he'd painted it white hisself!"

Rass had never heard Grandpa argue about the color of a sign, but he supposed Grandpa would have, for everyone always said such things about him. He said, "It is true that Grandpa saw Abraham Lincoln, ain't it? I told Miz Noelte that, and she said he couldn't have. But I say he did!"

"Did you bother tellin' her that he was goin' on ninety-five years old when he tole you that?"

"No, but I told her I didn't like her!"

"Let's see, you're eleven today. You're gittin' old enough to use a little common sense about folks that are over you. It'd be for the best if you didn't tell a teacher face to face that you don't like 'er."

"It's the truth! Ain't no use lyin' about it!"

Dad did not answer.

They walked another long, silent span of time, and then Rass said, "Colder'n blazes, ain't it?"

Still Dad did not bother to answer.

Hickman's truck went by over on the gravel road, and Pam waved her new scarf at them. Rass did not wave back, explaining to Dad, "I don't pay her no mind. She's jist tryin' to show off that scarf she got for her birthday present."

"It ain't common to give folks presents on their birthdays," Dad said.

"Pam's a spoiled one, no two ways about it."

"Rass, shut up! I declare, you could talk a man's head clean off. Now jist rest your tongue awhile an' stop breathin' in all that cold air!"

They walked in silence until Rass was almost to school. Then he said, "I need a tablet. I made the last one hold out for a month plus two days. I ain't got but four sheets left. I'd be havin' to ask for a nickel tomorrow anyway."

"Glad to hear you cut down on some of your wastefulness. I'll stop at Truby's with you."

As they entered the store, Dad added, "Might as well take your five cents for store-bought Valentines now too. I gave the girls thurs yestirdy."

"Yeah, I know! Sally already bought five penny-ones, an' Roselee said that Sally spent that dime Bertie gave her on her birthday all on *one single fancy Valentine* to give to Mr.

Pritse 'cause she just loves *rich* men!" He said all with one breath.

"Bertie's not got any call to squander her money on kids' birthdays, an' Sally knows better'n to do a stunt like that!"

They approached the big glass window of the little store that stood in front of the school. Rass spotted the large folded comic picture of a teacher that he was going to buy for Miss Noelte. It cost five cents.

Maybe Dad could feel his intent, for he said, "A penny is more than enough to pay for a Valentine!"

They went in. Rass picked up an Indian Chief tablet and Dad laid a nickel on the counter. Then Rass looked at the brown-yellow candy corn, the pink coconut bonbons, the jellied orange slices, and the little candy canes and the forbidden big ones.

"For the Valentines and this stick of candy here," Dad said, and he handed Rass two nickels.

Rass's hand reached out and closed over the huge candy stick. Never before had he touched a five-cent candy stick. What had come over Dad, squandering his money like this? It wasn't even Christmas and here Dad was softening! Right in the middle of February! Maybe Dad would be nice to him all the time, now that he was eleven.

Dad said, "Git on to school, you'll be late."

"I won't be late. Y'can rest easy on that! I won't be late!" Rass said. He backed out the door and then ran happy as a colt to the schoolhouse. A birthday present! His *very first* birthday present! Dad *had* changed, no doubt about it! He might just give Roselee Snowball for keeps, and he and Dad would go fishing all the time.

Rass carried the candy high as he walked down the hall to the coat rack. He took a bite of the stingy sweet peppermint and then held it between his teeth as he took off his coat. L.G. came down from the upstairs classrooms, stopped when he saw him and the big stick of candy, and asked, "Did you spend your Valentine money on that?"

Rass had a feeling that Dad never meant that anyone should know about the present. "Yes," he answered, and then let L.G. break a piece off with his teeth. "Don't crack it! Take it upstairs an' give Frank an' Howard a bite, too, an' bring it right back or I'll lay for you at recess!"

Rass tried to keep the good feeling going the rest of the day, but Miss Noelte was fussing about his not being able to find his and Sally's reader. She even called Frank down from the upstairs classrooms and gave him a good talking to. She kept Rass after school and made him search, but it did no good.

He had Sally help him search at home, and Mom joined in, too. A thing was as good as found if Mom helped, for nothing could get past her. "Did you look in the closet?" Mom asked. "Under all the beds? In the pile of wood behind the kitchen stove? Git busy, we ain't got no dollar and seventy-five cents in the winter season!"

No reader was found in all the search, and when everyone had to admit this terrible fact, Mom and Dad went out to the back porch to talk in private. Plotting his punishment, no doubt. When they came back in, Mom said, "Rass, you'll have to carry the Bard Rock hen into Mr. Raymond's tomorr. She's a good layer. Be sure to tell him that, and tell him why we need the money, and I thank he'll give us the dollar seventy-five."

Dad said, "I'll mark it down in my ledger and you'll pay me back, come cotton pickin' again. In the meantime, come git your lickin'." Guess Dad had not changed, after all.

"I didn't lose that blame book, an' I ain't gonna pay for it, an' you ain't gonna catch me carryin' no hen into town, neither!" he said. The look Dad gave him then told him what to expect all next week.

"We'll see about that!" Dad grabbed Rass's nice braided bullwhip that Willis had given him at Christmas, and cracked him hard with it.

Then Frank put aside the book he was studying and grabbed the end of the whip and said, "Hold it. I'll take the hen in."

Dad pushed Frank aside and finished the licking, and then put the whip down. Mom picked it up, then put it back in favor of the razor strop, and said, "It's got to be done, Sally! The book was half yourn, and we cain't afford such wastefulness. You gotta learn your lesson too. Come on in the kitchen. Spare the rod an' spoil the child!"

Dad said, "I don't figure Sally lost that reader; she ain't the losin' kind." Mom seldom ever crossed Dad, so she put the strop down and went into the kitchen alone.

Roselee, who had been crouching low and watching, said nothing.

Sissy asked if Mom was going to make Rass another birthday cake. Mom said, "Rass'll be goin' to bed without so much as a cold biscuit if he don't gin around and start keepin' track of his thangs. Git in bed. It's warmin' up out and everyone's goin' to school tomorr!"

The next day Frank carried in the hen and got the book paid for, and Miss Noelte gave them a new one.

The classroom was filled with the smells of perfume, candy, and Valentine ink. Rass got two Valentines out of the Valentine box, which was pretty good, since he had not put even one in. He took the cards and headed toward home, so he would not be around when Miss Noelte found the comic one he had put in her desk, and also to beat the cold and darkness home.

He left the gravel road to cut across the cornfield. As he crawled under the barbed wire, he saw a water-soaked reader lying on the exposed root of the pignut tree. Sally had been sitting on that the other morning! So she was not the losing kind, huh? And *he* had taken Sally's licking! Oh, well, he had not been caught other times. Dad would never believe him if he told. Mom would go into a sweat about the dollar seventy-five, and there was no place to hide the book in a family as big as his. He carried it to a low spot in the old corn rows and started to cover it with cornstalks, nutshells, and hunks of frozen mud.

Then Rass noticed a bit of cellophane sticking out from the center pages. It was Sally's fancy ten-cent Valentine, all nice and dry and smooth and still sweet-smelling in its waterproof covering!

He stuck the Valentine in his pocket until he got home and got Sally alone. "Sally, I wont to show you somethin' real purtty! Bet y'cain't believe it stayed that dry when the old reader was ruined."

The truth came to Sally immediately, for her lips fell apart and her eyes looked scared. Then she tightened up her mouth and threw back her head a bit and said, "I don't know a thang about what you're sayin'!"

"I thought you wasn't the losin' type, nor the lyin' type, either, accordin' to you! It sure musta been hard to keep quiet about losing your fancy Valentine. You want me to show Dad the reader and tell him where you was settin'?"

"Where is it? Let me see it. Maybe we can fix it and use it, and maybe Mr. Raymond will give our hen back."

"Aw, stop dreamin'. It was a total mess, an' I buried it. You're too big a sissy to take your own lickin's. Girls!" He threw the Valentine at her and started back to the living room.

Sally caught up with him and said with tenderness, "Rass, the Valentine is yours. I want you to have it."

"Now that's a dumb thang, givin' a Valentine to your own brother!"

"It cost ten cents!" Sally said and pushed it into his pocket.

He walked away, and when he got out of Sally's sight he took it out to look at again. It was a mighty nice Valentine. He took it into the kitchen and gave it to Mom.

Mom's face worked as she laid down the gravy spoon and gently handled the delicate Valentine. "Why, Rass, you oughtna spent your money on me! That was for school! It musta cost your whole five cents!" She drew her apron up in her usual way to wipe her forehead but used it to wipe something from her eye instead.

Rass left, for he could not stand to see a woman "carry on." Still and all, *he* had given a present! It was the first time he ever had. But then, it was the first time he had been eleven years old, too.

Seven

A year had passed, and school had let out for another season of spring cotton chopping. The work was all done now and school had not restarted as yet, so Rass, who was twelve this year, had time free to let his mind wander onto new ideas. He sat at the kitchen table making finger trails through some spilled flour and listening to Sally and Mom talk.

"If you ever got tard, I could cook!" Sally hopefully looked at Mom.

Mom slapped the stove lid shut over the hot coals and laid the lifting handle down with a bang.

"You can git them potaters peeled like you're told. Bein' tard has never stopped me from my work yet!" Mom wiped beads of perspiration from her forehead with the underside of her apron, leaving the top side clean to accumulate its own particular stains of food.

"Paulette Cross cooks, an' she's ten years old, same as me!"

"Look at that family, too!" Mom retorted. "Paulette's likely as wasteful as her mother! A wife's place is to make means stretch as far as they can! I got no place for wastefulness in my kitchen! Move aside and let me season them beans!"

Sally was going about it all wrong, trying to reason with

Mom. Mom liked to cook and that was the truth. People bragged about her cooking. Mom would never just up and let Sally cook. 'Course Sally was not as good as Rass was at thinking up ways, and she did have a problem. She was already ten, and she had to know how to cook before she got to be eighteen and married.

Rass watched Mom push Sally aside to get through the door and out to the smokehouse. "Mercy, look at the thickness of them peelin's. You'll never find a man who'll have you. Y'throw out more than y'keep. And you wontin' to mess in my kitchen!"

Sally hung her head, not looking up until Mom left, and then she tried to place the knife nearer to the potato skin.

Rass told her, "Wouldn't be so hard if y'used that little thin-bladed parin' knife of Mom's."

"She'd skin me alive if I got down her parin' knife! Claims she has to hide it to make sure she has one for cannin'. She don't trust me at all! I'll jist have to find a man who hates potaters or one rich like Mr. Pritse!"

"Let me sharpen that case knife." Rass took the knife and whetted it to a fine edge. He could sharpen hoes better than any of the boys. His own pocket knife was razor-sharp, too, but he was not going to let Sally borrow it.

With the sharp case knife Sally finished quickly, and Rass took the potato peelings out to Whitie's little trough in the wood yard. "Here, Whitie! Here, Whitie!" he called.

The fat pig came waddling up, and Dad followed. "That pig is big enough for butcherin'. Y'sure fattened him up good. He's gone from bein' the runt to the first pig big enough to butcher," Dad said.

Rass looked up at Dad with disbelief. "You cain't butcher

Whitie! That'd be like butcherin' Ole Coalie or Snowball. No one's killin' my pig!"

An angry, aggravated look came to Dad's face. "He ain't your pig. I never give him to no one. I jist turned him over to your mom for backdoor raisin', that's all. There's a right smart of difference 'tween cats and dogs and a pig! He'll mean meat on the table for quite a spell. Rass, I swear you're goin' to be soft-thinkin' as a city woman if I allow it. Mark me, I ain't!"

The thought of Whitie getting his throat hacked open and him running squealing and bleeding off to die tormented Rass until his insides felt all twisted.

Mom had returned from the garden and stood there with the radishes in her hands, listening. She said, "Hog prices are high if y'git 'em in early enough. I was thankin' instead of butcherin' we might welcome the cash money right now. There ain't no real need for much meat with all the berries and fruits and greens I'll have to can this year."

Dad looked at Rass and then again at Mom. "Y'been workin' on your mom, ain't you?"

"Mom's right! The smokehouse is chuckfull!" Rass was surprised by the aid from Mom, and he meant to make the most of it.

Dad shook his head and said, "Well, I could use the cash. Y'cain't git credit on gas," and then he left for the pumphouse to wash up. Dad always needed cash ever since he bought that Chevy last fall! Mom had sure picked the right argument!

Rass breathed deeply and walked back into the house. Wait until he told L.G. about that close call. Then the realization came to him that Whitie would be gone anyway. He would be sold and killed all the same. He turned to Mom and pleaded, "Do you thank we could keep Whitie for a pet?"

"No. Hogs are for eatin'. Only fools like myself ever let 'em hang around the yard. I oughtn't ever let you take that runt in."

"Couldn't you at least *ask* Dad to let us keep him?"

"Now cut that kinda talk out! Y'wont your Dad to kill him, or you ruther leave that job to someone far away what you'll never know about?"

Rass could not rest with all the hurt piling up inside him. He went to tell the others. It was not easy to tell the little girls, nor L.G., either. They all loved Whitie.

"I'll talk to Dad," L.G. said, as if that would help.

"Won't do no good. You can outtalk Dad on some thangs, but money ain't one of 'em," he told L.G.

"Where will Whitie's soul go when he's killed?" Sally asked.

Roselee answered. "He's a good pig, so he'll go to heaven!"

"Animals ain't got souls," Rass told Roselee. He wished Sally would not bring up things like that.

"Who told you they ain't?" Roselee asked.

"Well, y'never heard Preacher Hoyt say nuthin' about baptizin' pigs, did you?"

"I 'spose you've heard ever' single solitary word Preacher Hoyt ever said?" snapped Sally.

L.G. laughed. " 'Specially when you're outside chasin' girls around the churchyard, Rass."

"Don't judge me by yourself. Cain't you thank of nothin' but girls, L.G.?" he asked.

"Go ahead, joke and quarrel. You don't care if Whitie does go to hell!" Sally said.

"For Gad's sake, Sally, what do y'want me to do? Baptize

96

the pig? Gosh, I don't wont him killed any more than you do! We got to thank up somethin' more sensible to do about it," Rass said.

"I hate you! Git out! Git out!" Sally ran to the catalpa tree and laid her head against the rough bark and cried. Now why did she have to act like that, and make him have to think about her feelings instead of his own?

Then Roselee said, "Sally, I'll help you." There she stood with a bucket of water. "I'll help you baptize Whitie."

"Oh, Roselee, do you thank it would be all right? Whitie would never go in that bucket!" Sally said.

"Will you girls stop worryin' about his soul and help me figure a way to save his hide?"

"We can pour it over him," Roselee said, ignoring Rass.

"No," Sally explained. "Preacher Hoyt says there is only one baptism, and that is immersion! That means stick him all the way under water!"

"Why don't you try the horse waterin' trough. That ought to be good for a laugh," L.G. mocked. Darn L.G.! Making jokes now!

Roselee turned to Rass and asked, "Do you thank we could make him walk up a plank?"

"I don't thank he would do it, Roselee. Now don't worry, I'll thank of a way to save Whitie," he promised her.

Just letting his mind rest for a minute was always his first step in difficult thinking, so he sat down in the living room and watched a dirt dauber fly in through the hole in the screen and back out again. The late evening light fell softly across the wallpaper. No use thinking now. He began counting tacks in the paper. To heck with tacks. It was time to reason. Dad had not won out when he saved the kittens. He was sure he could figure out a hiding place and save Whitie from him, too, but in the meantime he had to get Roselee and Sally settled about Whitie's soul.

He switched his attention again to the tacks that held the thick, heavy, rose-covered paper to the wall. His gaze was not more than halfway across the wall when the great thought came to him. He jumped with delight.

"Roselee! Sally! Y'don't have to baptize Whitie!"

"We got to, Rass. He cain't baptize hisself, and he will go to hell if we don't," said Roselee, and she turned her watery eyes away and lifted her dress-tail to dry them.

"No, he won't. That's jist it! He is not of age! He is not of age to judge! He's innocent in the eyes of the Lord! Preacher Hoyt says babies are innocent, an' Whitie is jist one year old!" he explained.

"Rass, you are smart! You really are! I don't know why Sally thanks you're jist a dumb boy. You're the smartest person in the whole world," Roselee said and tried to hug him, but he dodged in time.

He looked at Sally. "So y'thank I'm dumb, do you? Well, if I was in your boots, I'd already be cookin', instead of whinin' like you!"

The next day was Saturday, and Dad always went into town for supplies on Saturday. As he busied himself getting the car ready, he said, "Might git your grocery list, Mom, and make the trip with me today. A ride in the car will do you good."

Mom answered, "I been thankin' I might go. Roselee could come along and help mind Sissy and Mary, and I could do some of my own pickin' and choosin'."

That was luck! Rass could hardly wait for everyone to clear out, because he and L.G. were going to build a hideout

98

for Whitie, and he did not want to waste time thinking up answers to any questions that might be asked.

Mom ordered the smaller girls into the car and turned to Sally and said, "You scrub the kitchen and dinin'-room floors while we're gone. Ten years old is old enough to scrub and help out. Git at it right off, so's it'll be dry when we git back. And I wont it done right! Hear?"

Sally, looking dejected, slumped back to the house. She moaned, "I ain't never mopped before."

"Well, criminy Christmas, there ain't nothin' to it! You've seen Mom do it!" he told her.

"I ain't, really; she always chases us out!"

L.G. yelled, "Rass, are y'comin'?"

"Sally, I swear I'm goin' to twist your arm hard if you don't stop makin' me thank about your problems when I got my own. Now slop some water on there and swish it around, for goodness' sakes!"

He and L.G. got the pig shelter built pretty fast. Rass knew it would not be too hard, for he had often sat in the small caved-in place on the ditch-dump, and knew exactly just how much brush it would take to turn it into a good roofed-over house. Whitie would like it near the ditch, for Rass had that critter swimming as good as himself.

They were almost back home to get Whitie when the chickens started clucking and the cats running to make way for Dad as he drove in.

Sissy jumped out and went running in toward the house shouting, "Whitie's gone in a big truck, and we got candy and Mom won't let us have any till everybody gits home so's she can divide it!"

Rass could not believe what he was hearing. Then Sally said, "Rass and L.G. are down at the ditch. They don't know

Dad came back for Whitie. What are we goin' to tell them? What was the big truck like?"

"It was a great, big, big truck, and it had a trillion other pigs in it an' . . ."

So Dad had sneaked back for Whitie!

Rass spat. That dirty, low-down, double-crossing dad! What right did he have selling Whitie? It was not just woman thought to love a pet. Just wait! Rass gripped the ax he had used to make Whitie's hideout and began chopping down every bit of weeds and grass in sight.

Mom was yelling now. "Sally, Sally, come in here. I told you I'd tan you if y'didn't do this right!"

Rass just could not take family living anymore. He went out to sit for a while in the chickenhouse, but his thoughts never got a chance to settle, because he kept hearing Sally bawl and bawl. He walked over to where she sat behind the smokehouse. "What y'bawlin' and takin on about? Whitie?"

"No. Oh, maybe. Oh, I don't know. It's 'cause Mom give me a lickin' 'cause I didn't rinch the floor, and I didn't know I was 'spose to!"

"Well, do it next time and stop your cryin'. The lickin's been over for fifteen minutes!"

"It still hurts!"

"Couldn't. Razor-strop lickin's don't hurt more'n five minutes. Don't look at it and it won't hurt."

"Rass, it hurts most 'cause Mom licked me without no reason." Sally's face had a squeezed-out, twisted look.

"It's 'cause you're a girl and she's got to learn you to mop."

"Ain't there anuther way to learn me 'ceptin' lickin's?"

" 'Course there is! Y'can learn yourself! L.G. and me learned ourselves to swim! You can learn anything you wont

100

to if y'got enough guts. You could be cookin' right now, too, if you'd learn yourself!"

"Mom would never give me the chance!"

"You'll have to sneak, same as me and L.G. did when we learned to swim."

"Mom says sneakin' is against the Bible an' it's wrong."

"The Bible tells you to do unto other people what they do unto you. Right? Well, didn't Dad sneak Whitie offn' us? You're mighty right he did! An' it ain't wrong for a girl to know how to cook, is it?"

"Rass, maybe . . . Rass, you and L.G. didn't git no lickin' when they found out y'could swim, did you? An' Willis didn't git no lickin' when he was home and snuck out and learned to break Ole Nig!"

" 'Course he didn't! It's what I been sayin'! Now Willis is workin' on a real ranch 'cause he knows 'bout horses. Y'jist gotta sneak!"

"But Mom's always in the kitchen."

"She wasn't in the kitchen today, was she?"

He left Sally standing there, her eyes alive with anticipation, and he could fairly see the plans forming in her head. It made him feel good. He felt like going to find Roselee to egg her on to sneak and learn to sew, and then to find L.G. and egg him on to fooling around with the car motor and . . . boy! No one could sneak his pig away from him and think that was the last of it!

Things did not go quite as fast as he had planned, but Dad and Mom were getting retaliation without knowing it. Roselee had not got a chance at the sewing machine, nor L.G. at the car yet, but Sally did make a batch of fudge the next time Mom and Dad went into town and left her alone in the kitchen. The only hitch was, she had not been able to make it set up hard, and Rass had to hide it out in Grandpa's little house. Then Mom trailed a line of ants she was trying to get rid of to the little house and found it. Things like that made life a little tight at moments, but it was interesting all the same. Rass was glad about Sally learning to cook. Mom had never ever made fudge, and he liked it. Today he planned to have Sally try doughnuts. He had had them when they went to visit Aunt Katie, and they sure were good.

Rass found Sally slopping the rinse water on the floor and letting it seep away slowly through the drain hole in the floor. "Sally, make me some doughnuts!" he shouted, and made her jump.

"You scared me! I'll have to look in the cookbook and see if we got everythang it calls for."

Rass got the cookbook down for her and started looking for doughnuts. Bertie had given them that cookbook last Christmas as a sort of family present, she had said, and Mom had taken it as an insult. Sally grabbed the book from his hands and said, "I'm the one that's learnin' to cook, but you can start a far."

The fire was beginning to take when Sally had the batter ready. She asked, "Did you ever see how Aunt Katie cooks 'em?"

"You know I don't hang around in the kitchen when we go over there!"

"The cookbook jist says to fry 'em, so open the lard can for me."

He opened the hundred-pound lard can, and she scooped up a handful of lard and wiped it into a skillet. Then Sally cut out the circles with a fruit-jar lid, and Rass cut out the centers with the vanilla-flavoring cap. Sally laid the doughnuts on top of the lard and put the skillet on the

102

stove. The grease began to melt and soak into the swelling doughnuts. The smell was right, absolutely right, but when Sally took a fork and turned them over, more grease got soaked up. Then she lifted them out and offered him one. They did not look like the ones Aunt Katie had made. In fact, Rass had never tasted anything so greasy. He spit it out into the slop bucket.

"Sally, I'm sorry I ever talked you into learnin' to cook. I don't thank you'll ever make it!"

"I hate you! Git out of here right this minute!"

"Here, I might as well feed these to Ole Coalie. He'll eat anything."

Sally struck at him, but she also handed him the plate of soggy doughnuts to take out. He found Ole Coalie, but the dog only sniffed at one and rolled it around in the dirt.

Rass called to Sally, "A dog won't even eat your cookin'! I'm goin' to the ditch to drown these doughnuts!" He put them in a sack and took them to Six Ditch and sat on the trestle and dropped them one by one into the water. It was interesting the way the water came up through the center and how they sank right straight down into the muddy bottom. He hoped some old water moccasin would come along and get a bellyache on them.

When he got back to the house, Sally had the fire out and the stove cooling and the mess all cleared up. When the car drove up, Roselee jumped out and came charging in.

"Whitie got turned into soap! Whitie got turned into soap!" she yelled.

What Roselee said turned out to be the truth. The company had sent Dad a voucher for just seventy-three cents. Whitie had been so big and fat that he had been pushed around and smothered by the other hogs on the way to St. Louis, so he got sold to a soap factory. It made Rass sick to think about it. Mom rendered the cracklin's at hog-killing time and used the grease to make the family's lye soap, but those were just plain hogs and not Whitie! Rass could feel his own flesh being rendered as he thought about it.

Dad was talking mad. "Don't pay a body to make plans to use a little extra cash. The truckin' company ought to be sued! Not a word did they say, jist a voucher, that's all, jist a voucher!"

Dad was grieving over money. Not one word of grief for Whitie.

"I ain't ever goin' to use soap made from a hog," Rass declared, trying to get Dad's mind where it belonged.

"There ain't nothin' wrong with good hog soap. The point is, I weren't sellin' the pig for soap, but for pork, and the money it'd bring!"

Dad worrying about money! Money was good for nothing but to lay on dead men's eyes! Rass went out to the chickenhouse to get away from the words. Frank said that some factories made soap out of cottonseed oil, so there ought to be a law against making soap out of hog fat!

That was when the idea came to Rass. He went to the smokehouse and got out all the wedges of lye soap Mom had stored there, and sneaked into the car shed and started soaping Dad's car. He soaped and soaped until there was not a place left uncovered or a wedge of soap left to do it with. Dad would know it took more than a sissy to cover a car solid like that. If Dad loved hog soap so much, he could have it, and on his precious car!

The next morning Dad waited until everyone was seated at the breakfast table, and then he thundered, "All right, who done it?"

The faces of all Rass's brothers looked surprised and blank, and he tried to make his face mirror theirs. He must have succeeded, for Dad had to explain to everyone about the car. Rass acted the same as the others. Frank and Howard reminded Dad that they had both been away and could not have done it, so Dad centered all his quizzing on Rass and L.G.

"Whichever one of you done it is goin' to warsh ever' whit of it off!"

Mom said, "Not near my milk vessels they ain't. I'm not havin' that mess of lye soap around the house to cause slidin' and trackin'! What a waste, what a waste! Y'ought to do a lot more to them than make them work."

"Now you let me be settin' my own punishments, Mom. Well, whichever one of y'done it will have to carry water up from the ditch, a bucketful at a time, til it's good and clean. Now you might as well own up right here and now, or I'll lay into you all the harder when I do find the guilty one!"

Rass never did own up, but more surprising was the fact that L.G. never really denied doing it, either. Dad made both of them scrape enough soap off the windshield so that he could see how to drive to the ditch bank and park the car. When Dad left, L.G. said, "Now, whatever made you do a fool thang like this?"

Rass did not bother lying to L.G. "How'd y'know I done it? And how come y'never told?"

"I knew *I* never done it! You was the one that was throwin' the fit over soap! Besides, it sounded like y'done it. As for me not blabbin'? Well, I been waitin for a chance to git the car away from the house out from under pryin' eyes to have a look at what's under that hood! I'll look while you're a warshin'."

"Oh no, y'don't. Dad said we both gotta warsh this car."

Rass dipped up a bucket of water from the ditch and slung it on L.G.

"It ain't goin' to be both of us taking a lickin'." L.G. slung water back at him.

They had one grand water fight. Being in mud was never as much fun as it was now, mixed with soap! While they cleaned the car, they spent a good part of the time sloshing water and messing with the engine. Then they went swimming, clothes and all, to get off most of the mud, and walked back home. L.G. went to the barn to his cats. Rass went into the house to find Snowball.

Sally was the only one home. Her face was mottled red and white from standing over a hot fire, and to his delight the house was full of cocoa smell. It was better than the smell of Mom's cocoa gravy, more like in one of the dreams he had at quitting time when his stomach dominated his mind.

Sally said, "You're wet. Better change them clothes."

"Says who? What you cookin'?"

Sally said, "I made a cake while Mom had the girls out visitin' with Miz Brown, but she'll be back pretty soon and there ain't time for the smell to clear out and the stove to cool off before she comes. What am I gonna do?"

Rass looked around for the cake and said, "How can y'be so dumb? How'd it turn out? Any better'n the doughnuts?"

"It don't look bad, but I slipped and poured in almost the whole cup of water when it called for a half. I got it hid in the smokehouse. I'll give y'some if you help me git rid of the cocoa smell."

"It's a sad thang to have to git rid of this smell, but I'll do it." He grabbed the kerosene lamp and unscrewed the top and started dripping oil from the wick all about the kitchen.

"Rass, what y'tryin' to do, set the house on far?"

"Use your head! There's plenty of ways to keep grown-ups from knowin' what they got no business knowin'! If y'wont to drown out one smell, y'got to use a stronger one to do it! I'll jist tell Mom I was startin' her up a nice far so's she could make supper right off, an' that'll take care of the coal-oil smell and the stove not bein' cooled off, too."

He barely had the fire roaring again when Mom and the little girls came in. Mom pushed the little girls aside to find out what was causing the coal-oil smell. Then she started hitting and scolding for starting a fire with coal-oil and for starting the fire at all. She explained as she hit some more that she was not planning to cook because they had plenty of leftovers to make their supper meal.

They all stopped talking when they heard cars drive up, and went to the door to see who it was. It was Dad driving his nice, clean Chevy home, and Mr. Pritse was driving his big, fine Cadillac into the yard right behind him.

Mr. Pritse had never come visiting to their house before. What was the occasion? Rass and the others ran out to see for themselves. Mr. Pritse was talking to Dad about his big old breeding bull, and Dad made them all go back inside, out of hearing distance.

Mom was terribly worried. "Here it is suppertime, and the right thang to do when rich folk come callin' is to ask 'em to join. Hope Dad has got enough sense to keep his mouth shut, with us havin' jist leftovers!"

"Don't worry about it," Rass told Mom, and before she could object he marched out to the front porch and called, "Mr. Pritse, Mom wonts to know if you will stay and have a bite of cake with us?"

"Well, tell her thanks. I guess I could at that!"

Mom stood real still, just staring at Rass. He walked past

her with his head held high and self-assured, as he had practiced for such important moments. Mom started to follow as he went into the smokehouse and came out with Sally's big chocolate cake. "Sally had a little time left over from chores and made a cake," he explained.

Mr. Pritse, with his gold watch chain catching the last gleams of the sunlight, followed Dad in before Mom could find out the details. Mom sent the girls scurrying for glasses and the milk, and for saucers to put the cake on.

"This is fine cake. Very fine cake," Mr. Pritse said, and made motions to loosen his fancy striped pants where they fit tight-smooth over his round belly.

"I believe it is about the best you've ever made, Mom, right nice and moist, the way I like a cake," Dad said.

Mom held her mouth tightly closed, restricting her chewing to short, fast movements. Rass wondered if Mom was going to sit there and not say a word.

"You're thankin' the wrong person. Sally made it." Mom's face looked as if it took real courage to say those words.

Mr. Pritse said to Mom, "You've done a mighty fine job raising these girls of yours. You should be real proud!"

"Yes, my wife is a fine woman. I couldn't ask for a finer mother to my girls," Dad said. If Dad was proud of being poor, then why did he enjoy showing off in front of the rich so much? Rass thought he had never heard so many "fine, fine, fines" in his life—everything was fine. It was, too.

Then Mr. Pritse looked at Dad and said, "You haven't done badly by your boys, either. You tell me they're the ones that put that shine on your car? Wish mine looked half as good! I tell you, money doesn't compare to having well-trained children! You've a right to be proud!"

Times like these did not make Rass get completely over the

loss of Whitie, but they helped. Neither Mom nor Dad dared say a word about the car, *nor* the baking, and if he went to bed right off while Dad was in a "fine" mood, he might miss out on a licking too. He felt triumphant and good. He had done what he felt like doing and it had worked out fine. He might just do something like that another time. He was surely capable of doing really great things, maybe train horses like Willis, or catch a fish bigger than Dad, or . . .

Eight

The next year brought several changes: Sally was allowed to cook openly, and Rass was allowed to plow the crops during the summer. The biggest change for L.G. had nothing to do with the car, because Dad still held on tight to his rights on that, but rather that Dad gave him whatever he could make off five acres of new ground because he'd graduated from eighth grade and was home helping along with Frank and Howard all the time. Who'd be doing what next was anybody's guess, because Frank and Howard had both signed up for the Navy now that the season was coming to an end.

Maybe their leaving was why the air had a strangeness about it, or maybe it was just that certain time that comes in the fall of the year when things that you know well enough take on a taint of strangeness. The weather turns from sunny to nothing. It's not about to rain, yet you can feel cold rain all about you. It's not actually cloudy, but cloudiness has filled the bones of people all around you.

You start to eat and you notice flowers on a plate that were surely there all the time before now, but you couldn't swear by it. It's a time when you know nothing for certain unless it is that not snakes, not wild bulls, not big fish, not anything you might do will get to Dad—a time when you don't even feel lighthearted enough to talk to a cat. What does it matter? The girls have claim on your cat anyway.

Rass began to notice that people were less talkative. It affected almost everyone unless they did things to stop it. Now when Dad got the silents he tried to pull himself back to normal by scaring the little girls. It happened every time. As for Rass, he chose to pull away from the effects of the weather by going upstairs early and reading some more in his Zane Grey book. It was a matter of making himself think about what he chose to think about in spite of any feeling to the contrary.

He was thirteen and old enough to make his own choices. He was no coward, and he was afraid of nothing. Like right this very minute he could hear mournful voices coming from the living room and he was not scared. Not one bit!

Those moans were from the little girls, and that voice that kept going up and down like a lizard on a tree stump was Dad's. If you knew what a thing was, you could not be afraid. If you didn't know what a thing was, then you just had to find out.

Rass went downstairs and saw just what he had expected. Dad was scaring the little girls with ghost stories again. Dad enjoyed scaring people, and Rass could never figure out why. It was plain ornery to scare a little girl—Sally excluded, of course.

Sally was eleven years old and big like himself. He had scared Sally at times, but scaring a person your own size was more like proving who was the smartest, and was not ornery.

He said to Dad, "You couldn't ever scare me with your ghost stuff!"

Dad never paused a second, but kept right on. "I'm tellin' you, that house over by Verge's and Bertie's is hainted. It belongs to city folks what just use it for a spell every summer. The rest of the time it sets empty. Now haints don't let a house set idle for long. Less than a week after them folks would be gone, neighbors, good reliable people, would start seeing strange goin's-on. Lights would turn on for minutes at a time, lightin' up the place all eerie like, and then of a sudden everything would go pitch black. So when you girls go over to see Bertie, stay clear of that house on dark, black nights. Now git to bed, all of you!" Dad made a move as if to blow out the lamp, a smile curling the muscles at the edge of his mouth.

The girls gasped, and Mary said, "Daddy, I'm afraid to go to bed! One night I saw a giraffe in the attic!" Little Mary was soft as dusk. Rass seldom touched her now that he had got away from minding babies, but he hated to see her so scared.

"I ain't goin' out in the dark to the toilet!" cried Sissy, her face white at the thought.

Rass said, "Mary, a giraffe couldn't possibly get in a two-foot-high attic! Sissy, there ain't a thang outside now any different than before the story! Ole Coalie's there to protect you, and if you hear any noises, that'll jist be horses and cows at the barn."

The girls did not look any less frightened, so he said to Dad, "Ain't y'goin' to tell them there ain't no such thang as haints?"

Mom spoke up, "Rass, stop correctin' yer elders."

Dad's face was wrapped up in a thinking look. "You mind your own business! These girls know there ain't no haints."

Sally said, "But y'said yourself that reliable people saw lights?"

"See, you was aimin' to scare 'em!"

"Rass, your mom told you to stop correctin', and you'll stop it or I'll take a switch to you."

Rass said no more directly to Dad but began quietly explaining to the girls, "Ghosts are really common, ordinary thangs what people don't understand. Take that house next to Bertie's. When Verge drove his truck over that little rise jist before he came to the house, he discovered what was haintin' the place. The headlights glared off'n the winders in sich a way that it got took for bein' lit up. Y'can notice the same thangs happenin' to houses when the sun sets at times too. Now y'know the facts, so git over bein' scared!"

There, he had told them the facts, just as Willis had always done for him after Dad had scared him tall with ghost stories. The girls began to make common rackets again, instead of moaning, and he thought they were settling down, until Sally said, "There really and truly is a haunted house over by the swingin' bridge. Emma and Paulette was playin' 'Annie Over' at Mr. Green's empty old house, and each thought the other was cheatin' by tiptoein' through the inside. Finally they met each other on the outside, right at the same time they heard the tiptoein' inside. Ole lady Moore says the house is hainted and has been ever since Mr. Green died leavin' his thangs there and no one comin' to claim them."

"Oh-h-h, Mommy, I cain't go to the toilet in the dark!" wailed Sissy.

Sally was too old to tell lies like that, and acting like she believed it, too.

Rass said, "Ole lady Moore is lyin'. She loves spreadin' lies like the way some people loves fishin'. Who'd wont Mr. Green's thangs anyway?"

"Ole lady Moore is a Christian and therefore couldn't be lyin'. She said she got it from good sources that lights go on every night at eight and Mr. Green sets on his porch rockin' back and forth for a good fifteen minutes."

Rass could not stand any more of this silliness. "I told you there was no sich thang as a haint, and even Dad's got to own up to that. I'll prove to you once and for all that that house ain't hainted. I'm goin' over there tomorr night at eight. A fact is a fact!"

The next night after supper Howard said, "We've seen L.G. hold down his share of the work this year. We'd feel better 'bout leavin' if we thought Rass was as big as he thinks he is. Talkin' never took the place of workin'."

"I don't just talk! Now why are you sayin' that?"

Frank said, "Cut it, Howard. Look, Rass, L.G., Howard, and I are willing to go along with you to the old Green place. Give you a chance to prove yourself."

Rass agreed. They would have to cut through Brown's pasture and go past the worn-out graveyard, which had only two tombstones left that could be read, and then they would cross the swinging bridge to get to Mr. Green's house. He felt a little queasy at the thought, and the fact that Frank and Howard kept on talking and laughing got on his nerves.

L.G. stuck his head out the back door and then returned to say, "It's purtty dark out tonight. Sure y'want to tromp across that pasture? It's hard walkin' on a dark night."

"I can walk miles in pitch dark! You wont to back out goin', L.G.?"

L.G. said, "No, but we're takin' a lantern. We wont to make real certain that y'see for sure that the porch is nice and empty at eight."

Boy, it was dark now. "I don't object to a lantern if it'll make it easier on you, L.G.," he said, trying to hide the relief in his voice as he stepped outside.

"Rass, Rass!" Sally came hurrying to get him. "Don't go!

Come look! It's a real ghost. Look there!" She pointed to a white form swaying back and forth just a few feet up in the air. For all the world it looked like a ghost.

"That ain't no ghost," he said loudly, making his voice stronger than he really felt.

"Then what is it?" L.G. asked as he joined them.

"I don't know, but I'll soon find out." Rass made his voice sound again as it should. If it had been just Sally there, he would have put aside proving that he was not afraid of any-thing—he would have talked his way out of it—but with L.G. coming up he started walking toward the "ghost." His heart beat fast and his breath swelled his ribcage as he held it under control. When he got to about three feet from the willowy form, he could make it out. He laughed as loud as a calf bellow and grabbed it.

"Sally, I got your ghost. Want to see us rassle?"

L.G. and Sally came running. He thrust the "ghost" into L.G.'s face and then took it over near the back-porch light so that Sally could see a white milk bucket and a strainer rag that Mom had hung on the clothesline pole to dry. The pole itself had been hidden by the darkness. Facts were facts. There was nothing to be scared of. Rass wished Frank and Howard had been out there to witness things too.

"See, it was jist a common thang that y'couldn't know till you had 'nough sense"—he looked at L.G.—"or guts to find out!"

Finally Frank and Howard came out with a dim lantern—its chimney was heavily covered with soot. The air had a damp coolness about it that made walking through the fra-grant clover pasture a pleasure, but that same damp coolness brought on a sense of foreboding as they neared the grave-yard. Rass looked to see if L.G. was coming. L.G. was hover-

116

ing and needlessly helping Frank carry the lantern by the bail. It didn't take much courage to walk with your hand on a lantern bail.

Rass walked off to one side. The place was empty and still enough to hear a cat purr. They needn't think they could scare him! He did not have to hold anyone's hand.

Howard made a racket and screamed, "Help! A grave jist caved in with me!"

Rass saw the lantern between Frank and L.G. rapidly disappear among the trees. He was all alone. Howard was pulling tricks on him. He walked slowly to the edge of the graveyard, worming his way through last year's leaves, which lay wet and rotting over the entire ground and matted deep against the underbrush. As he came to a path, he saw the light of the lantern filter through from where the three boys squatted, hiding from him. He gave no sign that he noticed, but went right by toward the swinging bridge.

No one had any reason to use the swinging bridge. Mr. Green had made it for his own use. It was not built well, and now that it was old, a few floor planks were missing. The cable felt frayed in his hands. The wind swayed it eerily. He walked slowly, feeling with his toes, moving along with uncertain, broken steps.

Ouch! That dad-blamed board was rotten! Rass held wildly to the cable and tried to regain his footing. The action set the bridge to moving faster. It was almost impossible to watch for missing planks now with the violent swaying.

Gosh, was he dizzy! Blast that Howard! Funny, was it? To hide a lantern while someone killed himself!

Rass was at the end of the bridge, but there was no ground to receive his feet. He jumped as far as he could and landed on the bank. There was no way of knowing if he had barely cleared or had had lots of room to spare. From there the short distance to the old Green place was clear, clear as a chicken-picked front yard could be.

Holy jumping catfish, there *was* a light on in the place! Rass stood and looked at it. He could not make his muscles move to go find out the facts. A man came out the door carrying a rocking chair, placed it on the porch, and started rocking back and forth, back and forth. The noise of Rass's own breathing cut out the sound of the rocking. Then he saw who it was. It was Dad! Dad, trying to alter the facts, trying to scare him. Well, let him try!

He saw the lantern light and heard his brothers having their own problems crossing the bridge. He was delighted when he saw them come to a sudden stop and heard L.G. yell, "Hey, look at that old man settin' and rockin'; it's Mr. Green, sure 'nough!"

All the boys turned and started to run.

Rass cupped his hands and screamed, "And look at the other old man rockin' away right behind him!"

Joy, joy, pure joy! His heart burst with the success of his trick. Still, it surprised him that a grown man like Dad would fall for it. Dad bolted from the rocker and ran wildly off the porch and away from the house.

Now that that was done, there was no need for Rass to stand there any longer in the pitch dark. He followed Dad in pursuit of the boys and the light of the lantern. Howard was holding the light high, and no one slowed down until they were well past the graveyard. Rass yelled, "You guys, stop, I'm outta wind!"

They stopped. Dad's face was as white as a load of fresh-picked cotton. *Now* how did he like ghost stories?

"You weren't scared of no ghost, was you, Dad?"

"No, I weren't. Not a bit! I saw you runnin' fast as the next one!" Dad *would* hold tight to his lie.

"I wasn't runnin' *from* nothin' but *to* somethin'!"

Dad said, "Cut the talkin'; there's work to be done tomorr!" He began to walk toward home.

Rass announced to anyone who would listen, "It don't take an ounce o' courage to set up a ghost trick."

"Yeah, but that was a real swell trick y'pulled on Dad. How'd y'think it up?"

"Oh, it warn't hard. I took it right out of another of Dad's ghost stories he was scarin' the little girls with onct."

Howard said, "I don't hear Dad laughin'. Guess he jist cain't take a joke."

It was nice of Howard to say that. Rass walked beside his brothers all the way home, but he made no special point of staying in the lantern light. The path was there, light or not. He was afraid of nothing.

Nine

The rains had kept up for too long the spring Rass graduated from eighth grade. A lot of farmers were left with short crops. In order to beat time and get crops reseeded, Dad went to Mr. Mac and bought a new tractor on credit.

Now Dad was even with Uncle Jake. He said buying the tractor was justified because it was better to be deeply in debt than to be wiped out. Besides, he needed a tractor with all his sons running out on him. Even L.G. had been talking a lot lately about going into the service as soon as he hit seventeen.

Against Mom's warnings, they had been working in the fields on Sunday, and the big fishing trip that they had hoped to make over to the Mississippi this spring was put off. The summer had been nothing but hard work, with no time for fooling around ditches or visiting with friends. One day Rass saw his friend Bud Mac in town buying school clothes. Bud had said, "I cain't wait 'til Monday. Summer's been long enough. How do you feel about it? Ain't you ready to git back in school agin, Rass?"

"Naw," Rass had answered. "I'll see you 'round, Bud."

That was what he'd said instead of telling Bud right out that Dad wasn't letting him and Sally go to high school. The older ones in the family never got to go either, although L.G. had talked about it for a while.

L..G. would know if there was any chance of Dad's changing his mind on the matter. Rass found him working at the endless job of chopping stovewood for winter. He picked up the other ax and, as he did, began, "L.G., why didn't you go to high school like you told Mr. Aaral you was goin' to do?"

"You know why! Same reason you're not goin'!" L.G. snapped.

"How come you never found no way around the situation? You always could!"

L.G. stopped chopping and said just a bit sadly, "I stopped askin' when Dad gave me five acres and all I could make on it clear. I liked running the tractor this year. Anyway, I'm biding time. The Army calls me." Then L.G. gave a care-free smile and socked the ax neatly through the middle of a tree section. He added, " 'Course, I quit before Dad got the tractor, so I was absolutely needed. If it was to be done over again and I wasn't so long out of school, I might handle things a bit different. Try, Rass. A No never scraped any hide."

Rass took L.G.'s words seriously. L.G. knew Dad better than most. He got himself set to take any reaction Dad might give and the next day he made his first attempt.

"Dad, I want to go to ninth grade. I'm off school for cotton choppin' and cotton pickin', and there ain't that much to do in the winter."

Dad's look at that moment meant at least scoldings for a week and extra work piled on as long as he stayed riled. Rass knew in advance the answer that was coming. "What makes you thank you got the right to go above your raisin'? It's that rich Mac kid puttin' on airs in front of you agin!

What makes you thank you're so all-farred smart that you gotta go on to high school? Y'got ideas of bein' a school-teacher? Hmph! You're stayin' home and helpin' with the early plantin' and the late harvest. You're going to help clear the rest of that new ground, days permittin', this winter. You got enough wild ideas in your head without gittin' more book learnin'. Rass, git in bed!"

Rass went to bed obediently as if he were an eight-year-old again. It was astounding, this power given to parents to trap a person. He turned back his thoughts as he did the covers of his bed, remembering the times he had hoped to please Dad and had failed. Once he had taken for granted that he would grow up and farm just like Dad. He had even wanted to please him by copying his occupation, but the more he had learned to judge Dad and his actions, the more he had lost interest in being like him in any way. If he ever farmed, he'd follow some of the ideas Mr. Aaral has been talking about in class, like rice growing, for instance. Dad was too stubborn to listen to new ideas.

So what if Dad saw only his own needs or L.G.'s needs, or gave affection only to babies? Rass didn't need anybody! He would show the world! He fell across the hard handmade cotton mattress and buried his face in it, feeling the buttons push hard against his cheeks, pushing out his hurt. Oh, gosh, how it hurt! Tomorrow—perhaps tomorrow he would find a solution.

But the next day he had not found an answer, so he walked into town to the little house of Mr. Aaral, the high school science teacher, and rapped hard on the door. Perhaps Mr. Aaral wouldn't even remember giving him a special invitation to be in his high school class.

123

Mr. Aaral opened the door, disclosing his small person, neat even at this early hour of the day. "Well, good morning, Rass. What can I do for you?"

"I come to tell you that I won't be comin' in your class. I appreciate your invitin' me. I sure wish I could come. Many thanks jist the same." Politeness did not come easily. It had never been a part of Rass's life.

"Why? Why, Rass? Your folks won't let you?"

"Dad don't see no sense to it. It's all right. I'm gettin' close to fifteen now, and in a couple of years I can get in the service. I won't have any trouble passin' the test. Frank and Howard did it easy."

Mr. Aaral looked straight into his eyes for a few seconds and said, "I'll help you, Rass. I'll come out and have a talk with your dad."

No! No! He couldn't allow Mr. Aaral to tangle with Dad. He said, "Mr. Aaral, you better not. It'd be wastin' your time. My mind is already set. I thank you again." He quickly stepped out the door and walked away as fast as he could without appearing to run.

Mr. Aaral called after him, "I'll come see your dad."

Now what had he done? Mr. Aaral didn't owe him a thing. Mr. Aaral couldn't get anywhere talking with Dad. There was sure to be a big scene, and for nothing! Why did Mr. Aaral take it on himself to come to his assistance? Then he realized that he had walked into town for more than just saying thanks. He had sensed this very thing would happen before he had ever started. But what if it ended with Mr. Aaral getting hurt?

When he got back home, Dad was out by the side of the house working on the hitch of his new Farmall tractor. The lugs cast sparkling reflections as he walked by. Dad was singing "Barbry Allen," getting most of the words right. He never had heard Dad sing any song but "Barbry Allen," and that was only on rare occasions when he was really happy. The tractor meant a lot to Dad; it caught him up with Uncle Jake.

Rass never said a word to Dad but walked on by to the wood yard, where L.G. was working. He picked up another ax and started helping L.G. cut stovewood again.

Chop, chop, chop. The sounds rang out from his ax and other sounds crept in between blows: the screeching of Mom and Sally's milk buckets, the calling of a mourning dove, the slapping together of poplar-tree leaves, the roar of Dad's tractor starting.

Then above all the sounds came, *"Hello, there, I'm Rass's teacher!"*

Good gosh! Mr. Aaral didn't waste any time!

The tractor sound cut off and Dad yelled, "What's that you said?"

L.G. laid down his ax and began to walk quietly toward the side yard. Rass dropped his ax and quietly, quickly followed.

"I said, I'm Mr. Aaral, Rass's teacher."

Dad's eyes tightened, the vertical lines in his jaw set. "Rass ain't in school."

"I'm aware of that. School doesn't start until Monday. I just came to make sure that he and Sally will be attending when it does start." Mr. Aaral's voice carried a Northern accent, but it was all kindness.

"You're wastin' your time talkin'. My kids ain't goin' to no high school! None of 'em ever has, and none of 'em ever will! I'm the one what says what my own kids'll do, not you, Mr. Aaral!"

"Well, you are wrong there, sir. The state law says that a child is to attend school until the age of sixteen, unless it is proved that he is needed to maintain the livelihood of the family," Mr. Aaral was still speaking softly, but his voice was firm and as set as Dad's loud voice.

"I need 'em home. You keep out of my business. Thank I don't know you? You tried to fill the heads of L.G. and Frank and turn 'em against me with all your highfalutin talk of science! Well, it didn't work! Now git off of my land!"

Mr. Aaral's eyes widened, causing lines to gather above his eyebrows. He bowed ever so slightly and said, "You'll find it difficult to prove that Rass is needed for support with your ownership of a new tractor. I'll expect Rass in school Monday; you too, Sally. Sally's a fine student; we'll expect her to attend high school too."

Sure enough, there stood Sally and Mom and Mary and Sissy and Roselee all gathered in a group, watching.

Dad reached for the sledgehammer he'd been using on the hitch. Sally screamed, "Dad, y'cain't! He's a teacher!"

Mr. Aaral stepped nimbly away a few steps, then paused just long enough to say, "If he's not in school Monday, I'll call again with the sheriff and a warrant." Then he walked rapidly away down the road toward town.

Dad kept shouting after him, and there was no fear or hesitancy in his voice, nothing but "I'm-making-it-my-way" sounds. There was no chance that Rass would be going to school Monday.

Dad stopped yelling, and the little girls stopped crying as Verge's pickup truck squealed to a dusty stop. Verge got out and lifted the new baby out with him while Rass's older sister Bertie gingerly stepped down from the high seat, her frosted nails displayed prettily as she grabbed the door for balance. "What you all doin' outside? Y'hear us comin'? I told Verge this is the noisiest truck." She stopped and ran to Sissy and wiped her eyes. "What's the matter? Will someone please tell me?"

Mom spoke. "A teacher is goin' to git the law on Dad if'n he don't send Sally and Rass to high school! Lord knows, we don't need no trouble with the law!"

"An' we ain't goin' to have it!" bellowed Dad. "Now git in the house, all of you."

Neither Rass nor L.G. had said a word since they laid down their axes, and now they both followed the others into the house. Mary ran ahead, doing a balancing act in front of Bertie. She was willing to forget the previous scene for the joy of a visit with Bertie and the baby. Dad stayed out with the new tractor.

Once inside, Bertie stopped and turned to Rass. "Rass, what do you say? Do y'want to go to high school?"

He was embarrassed at being forced to show his feelings. He hesitated for a moment and then said what he felt in front of them all. "Sure! Dang right I do! But what can you or anyone else do about it?"

Bertie did not answer, but she turned to Sally and asked, "An' you?"

Sally's eyes flooded. "Oh, Bertie, I want to somethin' awful! Miss Noelte says if I keep on workin' I'll be valedictorian of my eighth-grade class next year."

Bertie whispered something to Mom, and Mom said, "You kids, git outside. Run along, the whole pack of you. Y'all got long ears and big mouths. You, too, Rass, you got the biggest mouth of 'em all!"

Now what was Bertie planning? He walked back to the woodpile. The girls walked by him. Roselee, with head high, was in the middle, with one hand holding Sissy's and the other arm wrapped protectively around Sally's shoulder.

Everyone thought they could manage Dad—first Rass, then Mr. Aaral, and now Bertie. No use. It was as sure as the time set for milking. Dad would not let him go to high school.

Mom yelled out the backdoor, "Rass, catch that fightin' rooster and kill him for me!"

Things went according to company schedule. They had a big dinner of chicken and dumplings and then settled down for after-dinner talking. Dad sat in the rocker and began to read. Bertie said, "Dad, I'd like to talk to you."

Dad grumbled, folded the *Kansas City Star,* and finally sat up straight to talk. "Don't try to start nothin', Bertie."

Bertie stood squarely in front of Dad and said, "I wont Rass and Sally to come live with me while they're in school."

Before Dad could have time to react to the unexpected, Mom countered with, "I told Bertie it was all right. You got your tractor. You can manage. I'm not havin' the law on us. No one in my family has ever had the law on him."

Dad said nothing. Not one word. He got up from his rocker and stormed out of the house.

"Git your clothes packed!" Bertie said to Rass.

Mom said, "Sally, git that box off'n the back porch and come on! Bertie, Rass is sproutin' like a weed, so don't point out to me that none of his pants fits."

Gosh, this was a creepy feeling. Like divorce or something. Rass didn't mind fighting Dad, but this was different. He actually hadn't said a word to Dad all day, and here he was collecting his clothes to leave. He'd thought of leaving many times, but he had never imagined this quiet, bottled-up, mechanical leaving. Gosh, the power the law had! It was most unnatural for Dad not to say one word.

He carried his box out and threw it into the bed of Verge's pickup, the same place they were to have thrown the fish on the big trip that had never happened because of the flood. Thinking of fish, he'd felt very involved, but with this box, he felt as if it belonged to someone else. He was not sure he wanted to live with Bertie. He adored her and loved to smell her and hear her, but it would be like eating nothing but the frosting from a cake. It would be most unnatural.

Dad roared,"Git that box outta that truck. I'll thank you, Bertie, to leave my kids to me. If they gotta go to high school, it'll be from my house, not yours. I can take care of my own. I never took a handout in my life! Git them clothes put away, Rass, and git back on that woodpile. You might go to that high-falutin high school, but git it straight now: You're doin' your share of the work around here. I'll work you till midnight if the chore calls for it! Git movin'! Git movin'!"

Rass's mind spun past Dad's words over to the fact that he was going to high school. And he was staying in his own home.

He moved! He ran into the house and up the stairs, throwing his box of clothes over the banister. Yahoo! Wait until he told Bud Mac!

Ten

"Oh, give me a date in a Ford V-8,
With a rumble seat for two,
And we'll go wahoo, wahoo, wahoo!"

Rass tossed his straw hat on a nail on the back porch and reached for the washpan.

"I won't have y'singin' that song in my house. It's not decent," cautioned Mom.

"Got any hot water in the reservoir, Mom? I need a shave."

"There's plenty of water, but if y'use Dad's razor without asking first, he'll strop you, same as if y'was still little. The Lord says to honor your father, and that includes his belongin's. What y'shavin' for in the middle of the week, anyway?"

"Mom, y'know it's Halloween tonight, and the box supper starts at six thirty. A man cain't go to a party without shavin'!"

"Y'ain't a man jist 'cause you're fifteen! Y'ain't never a man till you've proved yourself with hard work and a man's actions! Now git out of my kitchen, so's I can cook. And mind y'leave enough hot water in the reservoir for the dishes. I guess it'll be up to me and Roselee to do the dishes."

Dad came in through the back door in time to remove the razor as Rass reached for it. "I ain't having no kid ruinin' the edge on my straight razor. That peach fuzz y'got there ain't worth monkeying with nohow. I come in to make sure you git it straight about walkin' with Sally. I already told L.G., and now I'm tellin' you. It's your business to protect her. I don't wont to hear of you leavin' her for a minute."

"Sally? I didn't hear nothin' about Sally goin'.'"

Mom kept energetically pushing sticks of wood into the cookstove as she said, "Preacher Hoyt wonts ever' young person out, so's the fifty dollars gits raised for the piano. We're doin' what's right lettin' her help out. She's already got her box ready and is rarin' to go."

"The whole thang's a bunch of foolishness," Dad continued. "Don't know why I'm allowin' any of you out, but since I am, I'm tellin' you to stay close to her. I'll thrash you within an inch of your life if y'let her walk that road alone at night. Raisin' a girl is hard on a man!"

Mom said, "You're goin' to have to face it, Dad. We got three more girls comin' up. Lord help us git them safe till they're eighteen and past the most dangerous stage."

"We didn't do so bad with Bertie—got her safely married off at fifteen. But y'cain't count on that with Sally," said Dad. "Don't you boys let your eyes off her. Hear?"

Dad sure never trusted Sally, and Sally had never given him any cause to act like that that Rass knew of. Dad was set in his thinking, and there was no point in arguing with him. Just the same, Rass had no intention of letting thirteen-year-old Sally tag along with him tonight. Not on a night like this, when he was hoping to buy Dixie Mac's box at the party. What did Dad think he was going to do, never be alone with his girl? And after Sally, it would be Roselee, Sissy, and Mary. No, sir!

All Rass's life he had been craving that special feeling that Bud Mac's cousin Dixie gave him. All he ever got from Dad was what was wrong with him, but Dixie liked him just the way he was. He felt great just to be in her presence.

It occurred to Rass now that L.G. owed him a favor. To-night he would collect on that by leaving Sally with L.G. He stopped worrying and began to hone his knife blade, razor sharp. He took the washpan filled with hot water to the back-porch stand, propped up the mirror, and started shaving. As he shaved, he thought of Dixie's springy little black curls and turned-up nose, and began to admire the strong line his own jaw had developed lately. He yelled to Mom, "Y'got the ironin' done?"

"No, but y'got plenty of clean overalls that's been wind-pressed," she yelled back.

That was not what Rass had in mind. "Sally," he yelled, "Iron my khaki shirt and pants, will you?"

Sally came to the porch where he was and said, "I don't have time. I git to go tonight, too, and it took so long to fix my box that I still don't have a costume thought up."

"Nobody is wearin' costumes, believe me. Not a single soul I know is. I'll make it worth your while. Here's fifteen cents, and I'll even carry out the irons for you," he said.

Sally took the money and then said thoughtfully, "Y'might need this money for tonight."

"Not on your life, Sal. I have seven dollars and fifty cents from pickin' cotton last week!"

"But that's your clothes money!"

"I know what I'm doin'. I'll git you a iron," he said.

He reached over the skillet of fried potatoes and hooked one of the hot flatirons into a wooden handle while he sang,

"Mama don't cotton to singin' in the house.
Well, I'll tell you, Mama, close your ears—
I'm gonna sing for a hundred years!"

133

"You're goin' to have to reckon with your Maker one of these days, Rass, so watch your spitefulness," Mom said. "Now git L.G. in from the barn so's he can clean up."

Rass left the iron with Sally and, walking out toward the barn, met L.G. coming in. "Hey, L.G., remember that time I lied for you when Dad got wind about y'gittin' in that dice game? Well, I'm plannin' to meet Bud so that we can go together to the box supper. I may even git to walk Dixie there too, and I don't want Sally taggin' along. Heck, I don't even know the color of Dixie's box, and if I don't find it out before I git there, then I'm in for it. Now I figure that as soon as we git out of sight of the house, I can head on to meet Bud and you can walk Sally on over to the school. Okay?"

"You don't give me much choice. Tell you what. I'll call it a deal if you let me wear your other khaki shirt," L.G. said.

"When are y'goin' to git your own self a khaki shirt? I worked to git mine," Rass answered. L.G. always had to push for extras when making a bargain.

L.G. said, "I'm gettin' some. No use buying 'em now. Uncle Sam will be issuing me new ones in a couple months. I took all the money I got this week and sent off to Sears today for shoes. Come on, let me wear one of your shirts tonight. I promise not to wreck it."

"All right, but you'll have to iron it, and if y'put a hole in it, I'll take one of your new ones. You're silly to spend *all* your money on shoes! Y'got any money left for tonight?"

"I got a dollar and eleven cents, and there ain't a girl around here worth more than that," L.G. said.

"Well, I wish you luck. You wont to know what color Emma's box is?"

"Naw, I guess not."

"Pam's is yellow and blue. No? Well, I can tell you what color Paulette's is, if that would help." He knew what most of the pretty girls' boxes looked like except for Dixie's.

"Okay. What color is it?" L.G. asked.

"Solid green, bow and all. Button up and I'll get Sally. I'd like to start early."

They all started off together. Sally carried her box in a paper bag, so no one could see it. He had to laugh. She did not even have a beau. Who would want to see hers?

After they rounded the corner Rass left L.G. and Sally and took the dirt road north to meet Bud. He walked in the weed stubbles along the side of the dusty road where he had mowed that very morning. Some of the stubs were a little hard for walking, but it beat coating his shoes with the thick dust and also beat walking in the long grass in the ditch where it would mess up his pants legs. He felt the unfamiliar tightness of the belt in the pants loop. Loose clothes might be all right for working, but tight ones felt best for dates. It increased his awareness of being male. He flexed his thigh muscles until he could see the ripples through the pants legs.

Bud ought to be up there on the ditch-dump path, and maybe Dixie would be waiting with him. One thing Rass knew: if she was hiding her box in a paper bag, he was going to have one good long look at it. One could not take chances in a case like this. Other boys had their eyes on Dixie too. Sam Owens, for one. Dixie had to be his girl!

There was Bud, alone. Rass was so disappointed that he found it difficult to greet Bud in a friendly manner. He tried to control his feelings. He had been practicing doing that lately. Dad always went into a rage when things didn't go his way, and Rass didn't want to copy that in himself. Still, he found it difficult when the situation had to do with Dixie.

As soon as he felt that he would sound natural, he asked, "Where's Dixie?"

"Already there. She's runnin' the plannin' committee, y'know. They're in there settin' up benches for the boxes and fixin' a place for the auctioneer to stand. I'd be helpin' too, except I promised to meet you. Besides, I wont to show you a nice fishin' spot right over here near the bridge on Five Ditch."

Rass hated to act as if he didn't want to know of a fishing spot or in any way offend Bud, but gosh, a woman could get into a man's blood until, in all honesty, nothing else mattered. He went with Bud anyway.

"Y'didn't happen to notice what color Dixie's box was, did you?"

"I didn't pay no 'tention. But she told me to give this to you." Bud handed him a folded piece of tablet paper.

Rass did not want to read it in front of Bud. Somehow it would not be right letting someone else in on their communication. He put it into his pocket until after they had looked over the fishing spot and then said, "I guess I'll jist set here on the ditch dump for a while. You go on ahead and help out if you wont to."

Bud gave Rass a strange look, but did as he suggested. Then Rass unfolded the piece of tablet paper. On it were three words, neatly written, "Gold and green."

Rass stuck the note down into his pants pocket. What a woman! Maybe he could be with her when the carnival came to town next week. He knew her mom did not allow her to date yet, but he would tell her tonight to meet him at the ferris wheel and then he would pay for all her rides. They would mingle among the thick crowd, smell the sweet beef being fried into hamburgers, see the colored costumes so bright as to seem unreal, and hear the sparkling sounds of thousands of happy voices as they walked together, hand in hand.

He never thought he would be looking forward to spending money on any girl, but Dixie was different. She was different in a lot of ways: Big blue eyes with dark lashes and black hair. What a combination! Gads, he loved her!

He had kissed her once when they had played that game at Pam Hickman's party. Lightning and thunder and little streams of water! Man, had he kissed her once!

When he got to the school yard, it was filled with young people, and more were coming down the road. Preacher Hoyt stood in the doorway, cupped his hands over his mouth, and announced, "Better come on in and git started. We're all gittin' hungry as a bunch of balers."

One or two started in, but no one was in a hurry. Rass saw L.G. go in. Dixie was probably getting worried about him by now—anyway, he hoped she was—so he went right in too. The spot where the boys always hung their coats in winter was all fixed up with bats and owls and spider webs. That Dixie was sure full of ideas. On the other side of the foyer, where the girls always hung their coats, was a young girl ghost. He knew she was a girl, because the sheet was pulled tight against her body; curves like that did not come on an old woman. In fact, Rass knew who had curves like that.

He walked closer. He took her hand and looked into the eyes he could see through the holes cut in the sheet. "What beautiful blue eyes you have," he said, tilting her head with his hands.

She giggled and said, "Boo!"

He tried to think of something very sophisticated to

say. "They're making ghosts prettier every year," he whispered quickly. He squeezed her hand and allowed her to push him on through the doorway.

He walked down the center aisle between the desks and approached two more sheet-clad "ghosts" who were arranging boxes on the display benches as they arrived. He spotted Dixie's box right off. In the center of the display, right in front of the kerosene lantern, with light dancing on every wrinkle in the cellophane paper, was a lovely creation in gold and green.

Everyone else had used crepe paper. Dixie was different. Some of the others were pretty in a way, and some looked as if they had been wrapped in two minutes. Some were pasted shut and some were tied with twine. Others were decorated with paper flowers. A couple had fancy bows. None could compare to Dixie's. Rass felt drunk with pride when people stopped to admire it.

The auctioneer walked up to the stand, and everyone found a seat and became quiet.

"Who is he?" Rass whispered to Bud.

"Paulette's cousin from over Berns way," Bud whispered back.

"La-dies and gentlemen!"

It had started.

"First, I'll ask any of you that wore masks to take them off. Someone tell the little receptionist to come in. The latecomers can find their own way in. Besides, it's kind of a warm night to stay wrapped up in a sheet, even if you are a cold ghost . . . yuk . . . yuk." The auctioneer spoke fast, but no one had trouble understanding every word. Everyone looked back as the girl came in from the foyer. She took off the sheet. It was Sally!

Great heavens, it was Sally! Auburn-haired, blue-eyed Sally! Anger flashed and replaced the contentment in Rass. Plague on Dad for ever letting her come! If Dad did not know enough to keep that little brat away from box suppers, then he would just give her arm a twist himself. He felt like going home. But he couldn't! He must buy Dixie's box. He looked at Sally, who did not appear in the least upset. She looked happy. Oh, well, she was too young to know he had squeezed her hand anyway. Still, it was a mystery to him how the heat that had swelled in him had not been detected by her, though he was most happy that it had not been.

Why hadn't he noticed her filling out like that before? He looked toward the front, where the other two ghosts were taking off their sheets, and saw Dixie and Paulette. How could he mistake anyone for Dixie? Her cherub face and delicate brows were hers alone! She smiled sweetly at him immediately and then looked back at the boxes demurely. That made him forget all about Sally. The rest of the night was going to be wonderful.

Rass pulled his comb out of his hip pocket and ran it through his hair once, pressed the cowlick down with his palm, and settled back to watch the show and listen to the strange voice of the man up front.

The auctioneer picked up a box, smelled it, twisted it around in his hand a couple of times, and said, "Here's a lovely little box. Who'll give me a dollar? Who'll give me a dollar? Come on, gentlemen; it's time to eat! Just look at this row of boxes, and a pretty little gal goes with each box! Let's get this bidding started. Who'll give me seventy-five cents? Who'll give me seventy-five cents? Gents, this has two big hunks of apple pie in it or my smeller has gone sour. Who'll . . . ?"

"Thirty cents!" came the first bid.

"Thirty cents here; who'll make it thirty-five? Thirty-five there; who'll make it fifty? Just like Mother used to make, and I'll swear it. Do I hear fifty? Going once for fifty, going twice. SOLD to the lucky gent in the second row for fifty cents!"

The auctioneer handed the box to Al Cross, and Ava Jones got up, and they both went to the back of the room to open it. Already the auctioneer was midway in the bidding on the next box.

Ten boxes sold fast, some for fifty; more went for seventy-five cents. "Who'll start this solid-green little beauty here out at fifty? Do I hear fifty?"

"Seventy-five cents!" shouted Wilbur Jones.

It was Paulette's, and L.G. was bidding. "Make that eighty."

"Ninety!" shouted Wilbur, twisting in his seat and biting hard with his teeth.

"One dollar and ten cents," shouted L.G.

That crazy L.G.! He only had a dollar and eleven cents to his name.

"Dollar fifteen!" said Wilbur.

Boy, this was fun! "One dollar and a quarter!" Rass called. Then he whispered to Bud, "Poor ole Wilbur must be about to have a stroke. Look at him."

"A dollar and thirty," said Wilbur, and stood up, with anger shooting from his usually dull, fishlike eyes.

"A dollar and forty," Rass countered.

"I'll make that a dollar and a half," said Wilbur, and made his hands into tight fists.

"A dollar seventy-five," yelled Bud, almost doubling over with laughter.

How could Bud bid that much? "You told me you only brought a dollar and a half, Bud."

"I did, but Wilbur don't know that. Preacher wants a piano, and he said we all had to give until it hurt, remember?" Bud whispered back as he raised Wilbur's next bid another five cents.

Wilbur finally bought Paulette's box for two dollars and ninety-five cents.

When would they get to Dixie's? Sweet, sweet Dixie. Like a languid cloud on a summer evening. Soft golden-brown arms extending from frills of lace on her dotted-swiss dress, short black hair bobbing and bouncing about her little face. When would they get to Dixie's?

"Looks like folks are really getting hungry around here . . . yuk . . . yuk . . ." said the auctioneer, rubbing his palms and reaching for the next box. "Who'll give me a dollar. Who'll . . . ?" He droned on in his unemotional voice. The boxes went rapidly. Rass did not bid again. No use taking too many chances. He might accidently have to buy one, and he did not want Dixie to get the idea that he was forgetting about her, either.

Some boxes sold for a dollar now, but most were still selling for seventy-five cents. Only four were left. The four prettiest ones.

"Take a look at these, gents, while the preacher adds up the money," said the auctioneer, and stepped down for a drink of water.

A lot of the people in the back were already eating, but they all stopped to look at the remaining boxes. There were the beautiful gold-and-green-cellophane one of Dixie's, a light-green one just covered in gold crepe paper flowers, and two white ones with big fancy colored bows. Rass put one

141

hand into his pocket to feel his money and the other hand into the other pocket to touch Dixie's note. He was ready.

"We have thirty-six dollars," said the auctioneer. "Loosen up those purse strings, gents. The good preacher here says we need fifty dollars. We won't start this beauty for less than two dollars." He picked up Dixie's gold-and-green-cellophane creation.

"Two dollars," said Samuel Owens before the auctioneer had a chance to start the bidding.

What? Oh no, you don't, Sam Owens! Rass straightened in his seat. He had seen how Sam made up to Dixie last week at the arbor meeting.

"Three dollars," he said.

"Three fifty," said Sam.

"Five dollars," said Rass.

L.G. whispered, "Dad would bust if he knowed you're biddin' that much!"

"Five fifty," said Sam, then took out his handkerchief and mopped his forehead and glanced at a piece of folded tablet paper he had in his hand.

"Do I hear six? Who'll make it six?"

Rass reached in his pocket and took a firm grip on his money. "Seven fifty," he said.

Sam wilted and shook his head No at the auctioneer.

"SOLD to the lucky gentleman in the fourth row!"

It was worth having to do without a winter jacket! Dixie was special!

"*Rass!* Y'bought my box!" Sally announced delightedly, and she came toward him.

Embarrassment, confusion, horror, and disgust enveloped him. He felt as yoked as Bossy with the forked tree branch about her neck. What kind of unfunny joke was this? What did Sally mean? He would kill her!

The crowd laughed. Rass grabbed Sally's elbow, twisted it, and made his way quickly to the back, not looking to either side. Words came out of him in a babble, but he managed to command, "Sally, go home!"

"We have to eat first. My box was the prettiest one."

"Look, I'm not hungry," he said. He glanced toward Dixie. She looked the other way. Next to her, on the side, sat ole lady Moore and her husband in a huddle, like dough in a bread bowl, passing along rumors, blowing up facts.

"But, Rass, I got potted-meat sandwiches in the box," Sally whined.

"Okay. *You* eat it! I'm goin' home. You come with L.G."

Rass left. He could hear the auctioneer as he went out the door. "Here's a little gold-and-green beauty. . . ."

How could one guy get stuck with such rotten luck! This was to have been the most important night in his whole life. It was just a plain dumb, stupid situation!! To think Dixie was his girl, and now she would be eating with another guy!

Sally should have stopped his bidding! He would see to it that she never went anyplace with him again, even school!

And Bud! What kind of a friend was he? Why did he let him bid on that dumb box? Surely he knew which box his own cousin had fixed. Rass laughed a laugh that sounded hollow. He guessed *he* should have known which box his own sister had fixed. There went all his clothes money on a stupid box. Box suppers were despicable, under handed ways to raise church money. It was plain robbery! And Dixie had made no move to follow him, had not said even one word!

L.G. must have known that was Sally's box. *He* could have stopped him instead of acting so innocent. Darn that L.G.! He was going to lay into him tonight. He couldn't stand to think what was happening this very minute at the box supper. No doubt Sam had won the green box with the gold flowers on it and was sidling up to Dixie. Blast that Sam Owens!

A little whirlwind whipped some empty marshmallow bags against his legs, mute evidence of a fun wiener roast had there by boys and girls who had things go right for them. Rass turned off the road and headed across the oat field toward Sam Owens' place. He would fix it for him. Lots of people got their toilet turned over on Halloween. That made a lot of work for the owners, who had to reset it in a new spot, and Rass had always considered it a dirty trick. But Sam Owens deserved a dirty dirt-shoveling job! Causing a man to lose what he had waited his whole life to find!

There was not a light on in the Owens' place. The dog barked, but Rass pitched a chip of wood over by a tree and was able to distract him long enough to slip by. He got a small limb from the unchopped-wood pile and let his anger surge out through his muscles as they strained under the task of tipping the toilet.

Good. He felt better.

He walked back toward home. People were coming down the road. He dashed ahead to the lane leading toward home and laid in wait for Sally and L.G. Hey! Someone was coming from the other direction, too. It was Dad!

Rass ran down the road until he met L.G. and Sally. As he fell in with them he said, "I've been with you all the time, hear?"

"Sally, that you up there?" Dad called.

"Yes. Is something wrong, Dad?" she answered.

"Thought I'd make sure Rass and L.G. weren't lettin' no boys walk you home. You're not allowed none of that. I oughtn't to have let you out tonight."

Rass gave that an amen.

Dad kept on asking prying questions, checking on Sally. He wanted to know who had bought her box.

"Oh, my box sold for the most of all. *Rass* bought it. I'm sure glad it didn't sell for fifty cents, like some did. I spent forty cents of my cotton-pickin' money jist to buy that cellophane. Cellophane is sure expensive." Thank goodness, she said the right words. Dad relaxed.

"Whose box did Sam Owens get?" he whispered as he dropped behind with L.G. He did not really want to hear the answer.

"Know that pretty green box with the gold flowers? Ole Sam got stuck four dollars for it. It was June Moore's," L.G. said.

"You're kiddin' me! Y'wouldn't kid me, would you, L.G.?" Rass asked. He paused, then asked, "Who got Dixie's?"

"I did. Last one sold. It was the white one with the gold-and-green bow. Got it for a buck even," L.G. said.

Rass whirled L.G. around and hissed, "I dare you to come out to the barn with me soon as we git home!"

"Rass, it's gettin' kind of late at night. Remember that khaki shirt y'let me barry? Well, that is the only reason why I'm givin' you this." L.G. handed him a piece of folded tablet paper.

Rass held it up to the light of the moon, and Dixie's voice like a willowy wisp seemed to tease from the page as he read:

"See you at the ferris wheel next Saturday.

Love,

Dixie."

A hot feeling surged through Rass. His steps were lighter. He took his comb out of his hip pocket and ran it through his hair and pressed down the cowlick with his palm. It had not been such a bad night, after all.

Sally's words had kept Dad from further prying and him from a sure horse whipping. Dad never used the razor strop anymore since Rass had gotten tall. Somehow he was going to manage to see a lot of Dixie. What was one night? There would be a lot more.

Eleven

The night at the carnival was the only time that he could count as a real date with Dixie, though he saw her as often as he could at school all winter. Then, with the coming of spring and Dad standing in front of a body with a thousand demands, there wasn't much use in thinking of having another date.

Dad sure wasn't ignoring Rass anymore, but the extra attention came by default. L.G. was gone. He had all the khaki shirts he wanted now that he was in the United States Army. Dad had signed the papers for L.G. against his will, but L.G. usually won out against Dad. As to any questions or speculations Rass might make concerning his own future or plans, Dad gave him the same answer, "Git on with y'r work and cut out the dreams!"

So he worked. But he did not stop dreaming. No man can lay hands on another man's thoughts unless he lets him. Rass dreamed of dating Dixie while he plowed; he dreamed of fishing for the big ones while he seeded; he dreamed of trying out some of the things he and Mr. Aaral had discussed while he cultivated. And yes, occasionally, he dreamed of some miracle happening where he would please his dad.

His muscles were sore and aching from all the work, but Dad was crowding him in more ways than one. One day when the workload and lack of understanding had come to a head, he went to Sally to talk it out. He found her climbing down from the cultivator. Dad had Sally doing a man's chores now, too, but he wasn't about to turn Sally into a man. No, sir. Sally wore a frilly yellow straw hat, big as the ones that came from Mexico. She had covered her arms with an old long-sleeved shirt of L.G.'s and wore store-bought white gloves to protect her hands from the sun. A sunburned woman was next thing to being a man.

Sally pulled off her gloves, revealing her long fingernails. They'd just about got her in trouble when she jabbed ole Bossy's teats two nights running. Dad had threatened to cut her nails. Rass could talk to Sally. She was feeling the pressure too.

"Sally, I hardly ever see Dixie anymore. She ain't the kind to stick to a guy that takes her to jist one carnival a year. I ain't been fishing once this spring. 'Sunup to sundown, that's a workday.' If Dad says that to me once more, I'm leavin'!"

"Rass, what's happened to you? You always got around Dad before. Why ain't y'doin' it now?"

"I ain't a kid no more. I ain't runnin' nor trickin' nor sneakin'. But the way Dad's been drivin' me ain't human, and I ain't takin' it much longer."

Sally thought for a minute. She put her gloves into her shirt pocket and took off the shirt now that the sun was down. She said, "The old way was easier, and you always got a good feeling when you won over Dad. It's the only way, Rass. You know y'cain't out-and-out, straight-over-the-table git Dad to change his mind on somethin'."

"I know that! First I jist want to satisfy my mind what's right, and then I aim to do it."

"Preacher Hoyt says Dad's got the right to make us do

whatever he wants. I talked to him. It don't seem right that Dad don't harr some help, but as far as havin' the right . . . You'd be sinnin' to go agin him."

"I'd be sinnin' not to! Preacher Hoyt can say jist 'bout what he likes that sounds purtty and like God Almighty from the pulpit, but he don't have to be crimped in by Dad's demands. He don't have to be hidin' his friends from Dad so as not to have 'em see Dad rantin'. No, I gotta figure in my own mind what's right."

"Rass. . . ." Sally said it slowly and almost as soft as Bertie. "What's happened? Now I know somethin's happened to git you this riled. Y'can tell me, Rass." Sally could be mighty beseeching.

"All right. Y'know that me and Dad hauled hogs into town yesterdy. I tried to dodge him, but Bud Mac spotted us and came runnin' up, his eyes jist shinin'. I knew he must be thankin' somethin' big and I tried to signal him quiet, but he blurted it right out, 'Rass,' he said, 'you ain't goin' to believe this, but so help me, it's the truth! Mr. Aaral went to some teachers' meeting in St. Louis and he told Dad about a professor who wants to pay someone to go up to Canada with him to fish. He's doin' some kind of study on fish. Believe it?'

"I said, 'No, I don't. But if it's true, what's your dad goin' to do about his business while he's gone?'

"Bud was feelin' real high about me sayin' this, and he says, 'I didn't say nothin' 'bout Dad goin'. It's me and you that could be goin'. This man wants someone to go up with all expenses paid, and he'd give us a hundred dollars for workin'!'

"I couldn't shut Bud up, and I hoped Dad didn't hear, but he did. I didn't even try to stop him—that would of been tryin' the impossible. Dad screeched right in Bud's face, 'School's out, and Mr. Aaral don't have no say anymore. Rass is home and there's crops to be raised. We got full-time work. You and yer ole man can play all y'like, but leave us that has work to do to our own business!'

"Dad was pullin' at me to leave and Bud was lookin' the other way so as not to have to witness it. Then Bud made matters worse by tryin' to say somethin' nice. He said, 'I didn't mean . . . well, it's just that it's a chance in a lifetime and y'know how Rass loves to fish.'

"And then Dad yelled so's anybody far or near could have heard, 'What Rass *loves* ain't part nor parcel in the concern of the situation! Poor folks don't *love!* We work, and we're proud of it. We ain't laggards or wastin'. Tell your ole man he can spoil his own, but Rass does what I wont, and he'll stay raised the way he was brung up!'

"Well, Sally, I ain't stayin' the way I was brung up! I whispered to Bud that I'd be thankin' about thangs and went on with Dad, even though half the town was lookin' on."

Sally said, "Preacher Hoyt said life was meant to be hard. But of course y'cain't go on lettin' Dad show off in front of Bud, even though y'cain't go Bud's way, either."

"I ain't so sure Dad's got the right to rule me down to the last say, with me bein' practically grown now and all. Sally, the time's a comin' soon when I got to act. I got to do somethin'. And I won't be sneakin' around when I do it!"

Rass left Sally to go about her woman chores and he unhitched the team for the cultivator for her and put them in the barn lot.

The next week it rained hard. No one could work in the fields, and Dad chose to take Mom and the younger girls to town to shop, since Mom was in need of supplies. Dad

150

gave Rass chores to do in the barn, and Mom left a list of house chores for Sally.

He got his chores done fast, spurred on with the promise he had just made to Ole Coalie. The old dog wanted to go tracking rabbits. He'd been left out of any fun too. So Rass and Ole Coalie set off to the woods, though he knew full well the old dog couldn't catch a rabbit even if he did track him out.

He said to Coalie, "Y' know, boy, Grandpa told me I could do anything I set my mind to. I'd like to set my own mind for once. Now the way I reason it, Dad ain't goin' to take notice of any idea I have, and he's never said so much as a thank-you. What I'm goin' to do has to be right out of me and I got to find someone with a piece of land willing to give me a try at it. I got a lot of thankin' to do, Coalie."

With the whole family gone, Sally would be baking, Rass thought when he went back to the house. Or maybe, with L.G. due back soon, she'd be whipping up some fudge. He opened the back door but did not smell chocolate or anything. Instead he heard a thump, thump in the dining room. There sat Sally with her head lying on the table, crying, and her foot kicking a mop pail against the old scarred floor that was now a hundred different shades of tan and brown.

"What's the matter, Sally? What's the matter?" Sally only moaned. He asked her again and again. Sally didn't talk when she had a mind not to. It took him a peck of persuasion before she finally let go and told him what was ailing her.

"I guess I'll have to tell you Rass. You might as well git it from me as anyone else. You told me y'was goin' to do somethin' But, Rass . . . Now Paulette refuses to come over to make cakes with me 'cause she says you might be hangin' around, and Dixie's dad says she cain't ever go out with you agin. What have y'done? You could talk to Preacher Hoyt. He'd talk to you, even if y'don't go to church." Sally's face was blotched with tears, and her short, thick eyelashes made dark outlines around her swollen eyes.

Rass tensed. Her babbling did not make sense. "Now hold on jist a minute! I don't have the slightest notion what you're ravin' about. Who started this rigamarole, anyhow?"

"Ole lady Moore told Dixie's mom, but she wouldn't tell her what it was y'done. Said it was too terrible to repeat, and, Rass, she repeats all sorts of terrible thangs!"

"Good gravy, Sally, y'know how ole lady Moore stretches the truth, and folks jist start subtractin' from what she says the minute she opens her mouth."

"That's why they believe her, Rass, 'cause she ain't openin' her mouth. Most of the thangs she carries has some truth in it, and now if her bein' a Christian is keepin' her from sayin' anythang . . . Oh, Rass, you can tell *me!* I promise I won't tell Dad or Mom, and I'll help you. I'll find some way to help."

There she was, beseeching him again.

"Sally, you're gettin' carried away with this. Now quiet down. Whatever ole lady Moore said I done don't mean that I did it. Folks around here has known me as long as they've knowed her, and I ain't worried a bit."

Bang! Dad let the screen door slam. Rass had not heard the car come in. "Well, you'd better git worried in a hurry. Come outside, I wont to talk to you, Rass!" Dad's voice shattered the veil of concern that Sally had been weaving.

Rass was not slow about obeying. He went right outside, forgetting the times when he had had a nice feeling of wanting to please Dad. He went out now not to please but to settle things. Sally might need him, even the fields might need him, but Dad did not need him. Dad only needed a workhand, not a person with a name and feelings. Dad wasn't asking him outside now to thank him for trying to make an acre produce a bale of cotton. To hell with obeying and trying to please Dad! To hell with honoring your parents!

Rass felt as mean as the white Leghorn rooster Mom had boiled for dinner last Sunday. He didn't care. He stood boldly before Dad and spat out, "You're the one what wonts to talk! Talk!"

"Listen, boy, you're the one what's goin' to be talkin'. And y'better start it right now! Tell me what it was y'done that was so bad a Christian woman cain't repeat it. Tell me, or I'll beat some decency in you with a horsewhip. I've been lookin' fer somethang like this to happen right along. You and your ways! I might've expected the worst."

Perpetual distrust! That was what Dad felt toward him, perpetual distrust!

"You always need a horsewhip or a razor strop or a switch. You always got to have a weapon, don't you Dad."

Rass did not move. He just stood there watching Dad's nose dilate, watching him shake with rage and lower his head to charge Rass like a bull. Let him come! Rass's stomach muscles were steeled. L.G. could hit him full force and he could stand solid. He was not afraid of Dad. Ugh! He held his ground.

Oh gosh, the saddness of it. Rass saw the rage squeezing up the weathered hide of Dad's face, the worry on the faces of Mom and Sally and the little girls who stood watching. He kept looking at them, leaving himself wide open, knowing that Dad was swinging. He felt the blow on his jaw, felt it

153

make contact and slip, but his hands remained at his side. A body oughtn't to have to hit his own dad.

Rass turned his back to Dad and walked over to the old cane-bottom chair sitting next to the washkettle where Mom had sat stirring the hog cracklings that she had rendered yesterday. He gripped the back of the chair until his knuckles turned white, and as Dad came at him again, he shouted, "Stop it! Stop, Dad! I don't aim to fight you. I'm goin' callin' on ole lady Moore!"

"You leave that old lady alone! She ain't done nuthin' but talk. If y'wont to call on somebody, call on your high-and-mighty friend, Bud Mac. Y'thank he wonts you, don't you? Well, Rass, let me tell you that it was *him* what told ole lady Moore what it was y'done!"

Dad was screaming the last words. Rass was getting dizzy from it all. Bud Mac? Ole lady Moore? Mom looking sorrowful and stern all at once. Aw, God, was it possible that just minutes ago he was out tracking rabbits with Ole Coalie? He shook himself into focus and headed down the rain-soaked mud road into town. He would see Bud Mac and get the facts. Right now!

He stopped at the gravel road to wipe his feet and wait for the Ravelle truck so he could hitch a ride into town, but the Ravelles drove right on past as if they hadn't seen him. He saw Mrs. Cross scooting into the house in a hurry after she had seen him coming down the road. As he got into town, women put their arms more protectively around their daughters, but when he got to Bud's house Bud came right up to him, not in the least mad, worried, or concerned.

"Y'thought about it long enough, Rass? Y'goin'? Say, is somethin' wrong? Your dad has got to let y' go! He sure is set. How do y'put up with it?"

Bud was still thinking about the trip to Canada, but that was not what he had come for.

"Bud, what did you tell ole lady Moore I did?"

Bud's face registered a question that slowly eased into a smile. "Why, I didn't tell her nuthin'."

"Bud, you know somethin' about this, and y'better give it to me bit by bit 'cause I got a lot of straightenin' out to do."

"Well, Rass, I didn't mean to mention it to you, but do you remember the other day when you asked me to loan you fifty cents so you could go and buy those bolts, and you was going to pay me back soon's your dad got over to where we were? Well, you never did pay me back. Mr. Moore was buying a new plowshare yesterday, and I reached into my wallet to git change. When I didn't have any to give him, I guess I said, 'Damn that Rass' out loud. Ole lady Moore came up to me wontin' to know what you had done this time. I started to explain to her and then realized it was none of her business, so I jist said, 'Well, it's somethin' I don't care to talk about!'"

Rass gave Bud's arm a hard blow of relief. "Look, the next time I owe you money would y'mind jist askin' me for it? Come on out to the house and talk to Sally. Let her hear it from you how it happened. And I'd appreciate your tellin' Dixie's mom too. Reckon there's no sense in talkin' to Dad. He wouldn't believe you. Besides, if he is so quick to jump to my sinnin', I don't care if he knows the truth anyway."

It seemed strange to be complaining about Dad to Bud instead of covering for him. They talked more as they walked along. When people started shying away from Rass, Bud said, "It'll wear off. Tales die out if they ain't kept stirred."

When they got back to the house, Rass called Sally out to the back yard and she came out while the others stayed inside peering out at him as if he were a stranger or something.

Bud said, "Sally, I didn't tell ole lady Moore nothin'. She tried to make me talk about Rass, and when I didn't she felt shore I was hidin' somethin'. She's got a rubber mind, that one."

Sally kept looking and judging Bud and his words, and then she said, "But she's a Christian."

"And she's a lar and a gossip," said Rass. "Now keep your mind on the facts and off the side interest. Do you or do you not believe I didn't do nothin' wrong?"

When Sally started sputtering and apologizing he couldn't stand it, so he walked away, leaving Bud to repeat all the details. It was nice to get things straightened out, though, and he had best walk back to town partway with Bud and allow Sally time to inform the rest.

As he walked with Bud they talked about the fine offer they had had. Bud kept talking about a week from Saturday, when they would leave. He let Bud talk, not confirming or denying.

He left Bud and cut over to walk the rails back home, trying to relax and think about his problems. Instead, just as if he had planned it all along, his feet kept moving right across the track and down the lane to ole lady Moore's glob of a gray house, surrounded by barren gray earth. He still ached with the hurt from Dad's mistrust. Why? Sure, he had pulled a few tricks when he was a kid, but never one against the principles of decency. Anger, longing, and bewilderment fought within him.

How could Dad think well of a woman who made a life's business of carrying tales, as ole lady Moore did, or of Mr.

Moore as well, for that matter? He was as henpecked as a man could be. It was shameful for a man to lower himself like that.

Ole lady Moore came to the door, her hair like grayed fishing line snarled from too much backlashing, and looked out at him with her little dried-up eyes. "Well, Rass, come in. Come in." She looked as smug as Ole Coalie did after he had treed a squirrel.

"I ain't stayin' but a minute. I jist come to ask you why you told Dixie's folks I did somethin' awful."

She ignored him. Instead, she reached her brown, liver-spotted arm out for her broom and started sweeping under chairs, even the one Mr. Moore was sitting in. Her dress tail was flitting with every sweep. It was green, poison green, greener than hog-liver bile.

He stood there and waited.

"I'll git to you directly. Here hep me move this dresser, sugar," she told her husband. She did not look at anyone as she talked. Mr. Moore sat there, peaceful as a toad behind a cabbage leaf. Both of them were oblivious to what was really happening.

"I ain't leavin' till I find out what I come for," Rass said and remained standing in the doorway.

She rolled her eyes upward and said, "It was my Christian duty. The good Lord says we're 'sposed to love our neighbors and it was my neighborly right to let a body know if her own daughter was bein' taken by trash. *I'd* wont to know. Bud Mac, who y'claim to be a friend of, was too ashamed to tell what y'done. Heavens knows, I didn't pry, did I, sugar?"

Mr. Moore smiled serenely and kept rocking. Rass said, "Y'oughta have knowed—"

"I know what the Good Book says. The Lord is no respecter of persons. Y'cain't 'spect me to respect you when you're carryin' on sich as y'are! Tsk tsk tsk."

He stood there watching her and taking deep breaths to control the words he'd like to fling back. She was a rattled old woman, and it just wasn't right to take her seriously, even to hate her seriously. Aw, he could not stay there any longer. He was breathing easily now, and this was wasting time. He stepped outside, and she continued to chirp away louder and louder as he put distance between them. Then she shouted, "Oh, Lord, Thy will be done!"

Rass glanced back to see her standing in the doorway in her green dress and holding the broom in arms stretched to the sky. A witch, a righteous old witch. He hoped she got bursitis to go with her religion.

"Boy," he said out loud, amused now at the sight of her. "If I'd done all the sins she thinks I have, I'd deprive Satan of his king's seat in hell!"

Still, his own Dad thought that way about him, too. Just what kind of person was he that people thought like that? Then he told himself to stop it. He knew what he was. But it was puzzling as all heck how a body like ole lady Moore could feel so right about her actions. Dad never found any fault with his actions, either. There could only be one answer: they thought they were right! It didn't bother their consciences a bit. Could you sin if you didn't know you were sinning?

It didn't make a lot of difference, though, whether Dad knew his way was right or wrong—it hurt all the same. It hurt awful to be hated, and it made hating in return come easily. Why couldn't Dad trust him? Why did he have to be so scared that things would end wrong? Scared? Big, strong Dad scared? Why, reckon he was at that, if you reasoned it.

Dad had to run things to feel safe, and that was bad, real bad, because Dad would raise Cain if he thought anyone pitied him.

Rass wanted to pray. Sally would be pleased if she knew. When he was little he used to pray that the Lord would make him grow taller and get more muscles than L.G. It was not until after he had given up prayer that that had actually happened. He wanted to pray for strength now, too—pray for the nerve to leave Dad and his ranting and dictating, leave him now before he started filling up with pity. . . .

When he reached home, Rass walked straight into the living room to where Dad sat in the willow-sapling rocker. "Dad, I'm leavin'!" he said.

Dad laid down the *Kansas City Star*. "Hogwarsh!" he said. "Sally tole me what took place. That ole lady Moore belongs in a asylum!"

"I know, but I'm leavin', Dad."

"I'll tell you when you can leave! Now git at your chores!"

"I'm leavin'. Now."

Dad just looked at him intently, never changing a muscle on his face. He never said a word, but his eyes spoke non-forgiveness and hate. It was Mom who spoke.

"A fine thang! Rass, you'll have to stand before judgment someday. All our worryin' and workin' our fingers to the bone, and not a pint of consideration do we git!"

"I'm leavin', Mom."

Mom's face was pained; her eyes were sunk in hopelessness. How could he leave Mom like this?

All the same, he started upstairs to get his belongings. "I might have expected this from you, Rass!" Dad called after him.

Rass wished he could explain to them. But why try? Sure he had words, but what good were words when the listener could not hear?

As he packed, he kept seeing the living room with Mom and Dad in their places, the furniture, their familiar gestures, all in bold relief, an enticement to stop, to apologize, to remain home. Then he walked down the stairs and past them, out through the door, trying not to hear Mom pleading, shouting, "Honor thy father and mother, that thy days may be long upon the earth."

Dad came to the doorway.

"Rass, stop," he said, "L.G.'s coming home. You're spoilin' everything. Why, I was plannin' to take the two of you fishin' over at the Mississippi floodway. Thank it over. You can check with Verge."

Dad spoke mildly. Was he begging? Apologizing? It was terribly confusing. Rass would have liked to have looked into his face for a clue, but he dared not meet Dad's eyes.

Instead, he turned and slowly walked back into the house. He had bided time most of his life; it wouldn't hurt to wait a little while longer.

Twelve

The next weekend L.G. was home, looking neat and polished and, for some reason, older in his army uniform. It was Sunday, but Mom and the girls weren't going to church because Bertie was coming over with her little girl.

The girls had the child in their arms the minute Verge came to a stop in the front yard. L.G. slapped Verge on the back and said, "That's a great truck y'got there, Verge."

Verge slapped L.G. right back with the same degree of happiness and said, "Well, I'll tell you, I'd trade it even up for your dad's tractor right now. I got no business taking off on no fishing trip. I'm so behind on my plowing now that I'm just seeding the best soil. I'm never going to get all my seed in the ground by June tenth if I die tryin', so I thought, What the heck, might as well go fishin'!"

Dad came around the corner of the house in time to hear what Verge said about leaving some of his land unsown, but gave no comment. Number-one reason, Dad was as excited as the next one about going on this long-talked-about trip and, number-two reason, Dad couldn't say what he really thought of Verge's actions without causing trouble with his daughter's husband, and Dad never lost sight of the fact that Bertie was happily married. Dad threw the huge seine into the truck bed.

The tension of the past weeks eased out of Rass as he sat cutting more holes in an old pair of worn-out gum boots, which had the tops cut off already. Dad had warned them all about the mussel shells, glass, and wire along the flat sandy bottom of the floodway. No one wanted to get a foot half cut off, so he fixed something up for protection that would also let the water run out.

Rass had put on his oldest work clothes this morning and now had only to grab a lightweight jumper to join the rest of the men in the truck. This was a wonderful day. No sharpness, no force, and L.G. choosing to ride along with him in the back of the truck instead of up front with Dad and Verge.

Dad yelled out of the truck to Mom, "Have them skillets hot!" And they were off.

L.G.'s eyes were shining, and he and Rass kept grinning back and forth at one another. It was really silly to be so happy. Then L.G. started giving him instructions on how to hog-fish in the floodway. "Remember now, keep your eyes open for signs of a stump hole."

"I know! Wait and see, I'll be the first one to spot a whirl-pool!" said Rass.

He had heard the story as many times as L.G. about the cypress stumps that floated in from floods and got stuck when the waters went down. The water had to move in a little circular path around it until the current worked out the sand. Then the stump sank deeper. After some time of this, the stump would be lying far below water in a ten-foot hole. The fish found that the hollow parts of the stump and roots were good places to hide in.

Rass and L.G. yelled back and forth in the wind as the truck moved along. Whew! It made a fellow lose his breath.

He crouched down behind the cab so he could continue talking until they reached the floodway.

The floodway was much bigger than any of the ditches Rass had ever seen. He waded in, clothes and all. It was only chest deep, but it sure was wide, maybe two hundred feet! The other men also waded in to feel the water and get their clothes wet. It was still a bit on the chilly side. You might be able to take off your long-legged underwear the first of April and go barefoot the first of May, officially, but sometimes the weatherman did not turn on the warmth. Rass got used to the coolness in a minute and then got back out to walk along the top of the levee looking for a whirlpool.

Verge spotted one. They carried the long net into the water this time and circled it around the sunken stump. Dad ordered Rass and L.G. to help Verge hold it upright in a triangle. Then Dad got into the middle to dive for the fish.

"When y'see my feet wiggle down there, pull me out," he said.

Dad dived under, but came up almost immediately, howling in pain and with blood running from his upper arm. "I got horned!" he bellowed. "But by jingo, there is a cat down there and it's a big one! Give me time to tie up this arm and then I'll git him!"

What did Dad mean? Quickly Rass let go of the net and jumped to the center. "Y'cain't give a fish *time! I'm* goin' after him!"

"Git back and hold on to that net!" he heard Dad order, but he dived instead. He felt power throb through his arm and leg muscles and work its way to his brain. He knew that Dad was up there yelling, and he knew that if he let this fish get away, Dad would take the horsewhip to him. But he was not worried. He was going to get this fish! There was no maybe about it! He needed it! He was about to prove something to Dad, something Dad could not possibly fail to notice! And he could do it!

Rass was big and strong, a full six foot two now, and he could hold his breath for a long time underwater, for he had been practicing regularly ever since he had learned to swim. His hand touched the stump and he worked his way down, feeling for an opening. Then he touched something soft. It was a cat, sure enough!

He felt for the tail and then worked both hands up the body feeling for the gills. Gads, it was long! He grabbed each hand into a gill from the outside and started wiggling his feet frantically. Someone was pulling him up. He had never held on tighter to anything in all his life. That old cat was not dead, and it was thrashing about, trying to shake him loose! He held on as the fish forced his body to move with his movements, and it pounded him again and again against the stump. He thought he would die if he stayed under a second longer, but even if he did, he would not let loose!

Rass felt more hands pulling at his legs. He was up, and L.G. and Verge were wrapping the net every which way around the biggest catfish he had ever seen! Dad was like a madman, jumping and hollering orders from the side, with his arm swishing blood into the water near him.

"Don't let him loose!" he was screaming. "Don't let him git loose!" He must have said it twenty times.

Other words were churning inside Rass. Don't anyone call me a boy again! Don't ever try to order me around . . . anyone . . . not Dad, nor anyone! That, no doubt, is the biggest cat ever caught by anybody!

He forced his tired legs to move across the current, and at last he stood on the bank. He watched them drag the great fish toward the truck. This was it! Ever since he was eight years old he had anticipated this moment—this moment of knowing he had earned acclaim. It should be the Fourth of July. There should be fireworks today!

Rass sat down and held his head against his knees. He felt the trembling in his body ease out. Then, after a couple of good breaths, he got up and ran about like a wild creature breathing the air of freedom. That was *his* fish they were loading! He ran over and helped them heave the squirming, netted bulk into the truck bed.

Dad said, "Well, that spoils any fishin' for the rest of us! Got to git home and round up the neighbors! There's enough meat here for the whole countryside! Catchin' any more fish would jist be wasteful! Fish cain't keep more'n three days!"

It was all right with Rass. He was ready to go home right now. He said, "L.G., let's git in back!" .He was not going to leave the fish. He sat and stared at that whopper all the way home, running his fingers from one end of it to the other. The skin felt velvety where the wind had dried it.

L.G. said, "I guess Jonah *could* have lived in a whale. I could almost fit in this cat's mouth myself. Dang you, Rass! I'm older'n you! I oughta got to dive for it!"

Rass shoved L.G. closer to the fish and laughed as L.G. pulled back. The fish was helpless enough now, lying there in the truck bed, breathing its last few breaths. Not a drop of blood on him, but death was all about him. His eyes were milking over and the whiskers had stopped quivering. It had to take a real man to win against a monster like that! Everyone would acknowledge that. Even Dad!

The truck stopped just a quarter of a mile before they got home. Dad got out and came back to the truck bed and said, "Keep your mouths shut, an' let me handle this when

165

we git home. We're goin' to have a little fun with the womenfolk."

Why not? Let Dad have a little fun, since he had no claims on catching the fish. They pulled into the yard, and Sally and Roselee came running out asking to see all the fish. Dad motioned to them to follow and then walked toward the back porch with his shoulders rounded and his head lowered.

Mom and Bertie came out. "Didn't y'git any fish?" Bertie asked expectantly.

"Jist one," Dad said pathetically. Boy, was he putting on a show! It was nice to see Dad like this, but the show would be all for Rass when they found out who had *caught* the fish!

"Then why'd you come home so early? It ain't even dark yet," said Mom.

Dad straightened up, whipped around, and shouted, "Rass, what y'standin' there for? Go git the cotton scales. Bring the ten-pound pea! Let's show the women what we caught!"

What did Dad mean, "we"?

Mom dropped her dishcloth, and she and Bertie ran toward them. He could smell Bertie's perfume. The little girls came flying behind them.

Dad hooked the scales over the low limb of the catalpa tree. The fish weighed forty-three pounds! Its head was a foot wide and it was longer than twelve-year-old Roselee.

Sally kept standing there, telling Rass how nice it was that he and Dad had caught the biggest fish in the world. Rass kept waiting for Dad to correct her and give him credit. He waited, and waited some more. His ears began to itch, a muscle jumped in his arm.

"What do you mean? I caught that fish by myself!"

166

No one heard him. No one listened to anyone else when Dad was speaking.

Rass listened to what Dad was telling Mom and Bertie. Dad said, "I spotted that huge cat and fought it until it was all tired out—and all the while me horned and bleedin' and smartin'. But I kept fightin' until I needed air, and then Rass had to come and help land it!"

He would have liked to have thought Dad was dumb. Dad was not dumb. It must have taken Dad all the way home to think up something as slick-sounding as this! Dad knew that fish had not been worn out. But he guessed just he and Dad knew that for sure.

Still, Verge and L.G. had called it his fish. They knew!

People kept saying that he should honor his father. Well, why couldn't his father honor him just once? Never again would he try. No! He *would* leave home before he would take that kind of stuff any longer.

L.G. must have sensed his anger, for he winked and said, "Let Dad have his talk, Rass, he needs it more than you. Won't hurt anything." L.G. humoring Dad? The service sure had changed him.

What the heck. Forget Dad. It did matter, though, to have Bud know that the fish was his. Bud would be glad for him. He sure hoped so, anyway, because that was the way it was with a real friend. They were glad for you and didn't try to hog your glory. But how was he going to get Bud here to see it? Dad would be cutting the fish up and Mom would be frying it before he would have time to get to town and back. Dad would get mad for sure if Bud came on the place.

If they could only get it stuffed. Then he would not say anymore about who had caught the fish. Maybe Dad would listen. "It's plenty big enough to stuff, ain't it, Dad? Could we save the skin and head someway and still have the meat to eat?"

"Straighten up, Rass, and stop your dreamin'! That's a waste of good money, which we ain't got! Better look at it all y'wont right now, 'cause we better get it cleaned and cooked right away!"

There was no point in talking to Dad further, but maybe he could think of something. If only one of the neighbors owned a camera, but he knew none of them did.

Mom did not waste time on admiring the fish; it was not her way. One could tell, though, that she was happy to have the meat. She yelled for Sally and Roselee to bring in more cookstove wood and told Dad, "Go git the Browns and the Hickmans and the Crosses and Preacher Hoyt. Lucky for us, the cool weather's kept up a little. If we git it all fried up, I thank it'll keep for a good three days. I never knew of anyone from these parts havin' luck cannin' fish, but Miz Brown may know. She's got a sister up in Michigan that cans 'most anything, she says."

Dad said, "Now calm down! I thank Verge can round up the neighbors! These boys here wouldn't know how to commence to cut up a fish of this size! It's got to be cut into steaks, and that's man's work!"

Dad was interested only in himself. Rass could never feel the same about him again. He kept trying to think of some way to get proof of the fish to Bud as he helped move the hog-cleaning block near the woodpile and sharpened the butcher knives. It was something to see the insides when Dad laid the fish open. He pulled out the huge bladder and gave it to Mary to use as a float in the watering trough. Mom and Sally brought out every pan they owned to collect the

168

pieces, and Roselee and Sissy kept pumping water for washing. Then it came to Rass how he could show Bud!

Mrs. Brown drove up, but told Mom she did not know if her sister ever canned fish. She said folks didn't usually get so much at one time, but that she sure had a choice recipe for catfish-head soup.

Mom called, "Bring that head to the pump an' git it cleaned!"

Dad was annoyed at the bother right in the middle of his work, and even more annoyed when he could not locate the head.

"Now, where in the thunderation is that head! It's too big to misplace!" Dad yelled.

Rass answered, "It's over in the pumphouse, in a potato sack under the milk trough. I'm keeping it cool. I'm taking it to town with me!"

Dad hesitated. Hesitation from Dad was a sure sign that Rass had a chance—and anyway, Dad must know that he was determined. Till now, Dad had run his whole life, and it just had to stop! Let Dad tell the neighbors what he wished about who caught the fish, but he was going to let the truth be known to his friends.

Dad looked as if he were trying to read Rass's mind.

Rass stood his full six feet two inches and squared his shoulders. "Dad, I'm showing *my* fish in town. I ain't saying a word here at home. Hear? I'm taking the head to town!"

Dad never changed his face a whit, but called to Mom, "I ain't messin' with the head. We got plenty of good meat here without chewing on the bones. 'Sides, it spoils good fish to make it up in soup."

Mom never forced the issue. She had the stove fairly dancing it was so hot, and already it kept both her and Mrs. Brown busy turning one piece of fish after another as they reached the right stage of golden brownness. L.G. was trying to swipe a taste, and Mom swatted his hand, saying, "Git out of the kitchen. The army ain't taught you any manners yet, I see. No one's gettin' any till the whole batch is fried up and that'll be some time to come."

Verge gave Bertie a little squeeze around the waist and said, "In that case, I guess we might as well go to town and buy some sody pop to go with this big dinner." The girls, who had seemed busy at play with their little niece, all piped up at once with hurrays.

As L.G. and Verge and Rass headed for the truck, Dad grumbled something, and L.G. said he'd just as soon stay behind and give Dad a hand. Verge waited for Rass to load the fish head into the truck bed and then spun out of the yard in a whirl of dust. "Yep, Rass, you got yourself something there that's really worth showing."

"Dad didn't make such a point of calling it mine."

"Ah, he was just kidding a little. He knows it was you that outstripped that cat."

Rass didn't care to argue the point with Verge because Verge was not the sort to look for trouble and he often tried to shush up things that were stirring. "Verge, Dad's been working us like mules and we're ahead of every farmer around. With the tractor, our crops will be laid by good and early. I might come over and give you a hand if you're really stuck."

"We got no witness to it, but I'm holdin' you to your word. Man, I could sure use the help, and I couldn't ever ask Bertie to be a fieldhand like some of the young guys are askin' of their wives."

"Yeah, and Dad of Sally. Verge, it's startin' to git to me the way Dad . . ."

Verge started whistling, so Rass said no more. As soon as they got into town he let Verge go after the soda pop alone while he went in search of Bud Mac.

Bud almost died when he opened the sack and saw that monstrous head and those milky eyes glaring back at him. He hollered and hit Rass across the back and laughed some more when his dad and two other men came to look.

Bud said, "Mr. Aaral. That's who we got to show it to. Mr. Aaral!" Bud took off, dragging the sack behind him.

"Hey, let me grab a hold. You wont to beat it beyond recognition?"

Mr. Aaral was impressed—every bit as impressed as Rass had hoped he would be. And questions—why, it kept him busy for a good thirty minutes just answering questions. What was the art of the catch? Where was the hole located? What was in the fish's belly when it was opened? Yes, indeed, Mr. Aaral was impressed. It was like a punishment to have to take leave of him and Bud and go back to where Verge was loading the soda pop.

Verge wasn't moving about at all, just standing there by the truck glaring at the people gathered in front of Mr. Raymond's store.

It was Dad and L.G. and about four or five other men. Rass walked closer. No one turned to look as he neared, for everyone was listening to Dad.

". . . Stinger hit me right about here. Toughest cat I ever fought. Of course, with a bad arm I had to git my boy to give me a little help. It fought. . . ."

Rass walked away, back toward Verge and the truck. No decision had to be made, for he had made it last week. He

171

glanced back to see L.G. looking in his direction with a troubled frown. Verge opened the truck door. "Rass, I might, in fact, use your help plowing right now if y'had a mind."

"I got a mind. Verge, are you really jist letting your shallow spots lay out? Y'really don't plan to seed 'em?"

"I know I ought to, but look, even with you helpin', I'm lucky if I make . . . ."

"Would y'drive around the block and stop at Mr. Aaral's? I got to see him for a minute."

And a minute was all it took. Mr. Aaral did not seem in the least surprised that Rass was leaving home and was very pleased that Rass would continue going to school from Verge's. It wouldn't be any farther to walk from Verge's in one direction than it had been to walk from Dad's in the other.

And right on the spot, without further discussion, Mr. Aaral placed a long-distance telephone call and ordered the beginnings of the first rice planting to be done in southeast Missouri. Mr. Aaral said he'd deliver the order to Rass himself. The way he acted you'd think that starting rice farming in that section of the country was even bigger than catching the big cat.

They went back home and ate lots of fish and talked ever so natural until it got time for Bertie and Verge to leave. Then Rass threw a bundle of clothes in the truck and got in the cab with them. L.G. made some move to talk but looked at Dad and decided not to.

Mom said, "Bertie, y'can use the extra hand around the house with you expectin' agin."

Rass saw Dad turning to go back into the house and heard Mary asking, "What is Bertie expectin'? Ain't Rass never goin' to come back?"

Rass thought it seemed a short drive over to Verge's, for his head was spinning with plans. Actually, it was a renewal of plans that he had thought out long ago, but this time with a difference, for he was going to put them into action.

Action and more action. Rass thought that he had worked hard before, but now he worked with a special vigor. By June 10 Verge not only had all the seed he'd planned for in the ground, but all the shallows had been reflooded and planted in rice. People around town whispered and talked about it, and there was no doubt that the talk leaked back to Dad, but Rass heard not one word from him. Bertie and Verge went over to visit twice, once more in the summer and again in the fall, but Rass did not go either time, saying he had lots of work to do.

He missed the girls and Mom. Sometimes as he worked he thought of Mom, wondering how she managed and why she stayed with Dad. Mom was bossy and harsh, but she took care of her affairs and still had time to let it be known to people once in a while that they were wanted.

It would have been easier if Mom had married someone like Uncle Jake. What had she ever seen in Dad? Maybe she just refused to let him wear on her nerves. Maybe she had found the one thing in Dad that had value and thought only about that. Could it be the same way with Dad? Did he have things that he centered his thoughts on?

Rass didn't care to do any more thinking about it. The last time he had tried understanding Dad was the time he had started to pity him.

The rice crop was harvested and the money was in Rass's pocket. Bertie and Verge had their harvest money, too, and were busy planning a shopping trip before they went home to Dad and Mom's for Christmas. Rass had told them he might like to send along some presents for the girls, but he wouldn't be going himself.

Bertie had ordered most of her wants from the Sears catalog and was running down to the mailbox now to collect her package. She came running back calling, "Rass, it's a letter for you from Dad. Read it. Well, go ahead and read it. What does he say?"

Rass knew before he opened the letter that it would not be a full page. Dad always wrote half-page letters to Willis, Frank, Howard, and L.G.

Dear Rass,

We're fine. Cain't complain. Sally has made a good fieldhand. The crops were as good as could be expected.

Willis thanks he'll make it home agin for Christmas.

Frank and Howard and L.G. are all gettin' leaves from service. Cain't say that I thank much fur thur choice of work. Don't take much sense to be in service. I got to close now and chop wood. If you git tard playin' and experimentin', thur is still plenty of work to be done.

Mom hopes y'll git home, too.

As ever,

Dad.

Play? Why, he'd worked harder and made more money this season than he had in three seasons at home! Dad wouldn't take notice to a new idea, a new way. He couldn't.

174

His way was the only way he knew and the only way he could make a sensible judgment on.

Mom wants me to come home, but do you, Dad? Rass folded the letter and put it into his pocket and began to smile. Dad took constant thinking. He couldn't say things right out, and never would. Figuring people out was a hard chore if you really set your mind on doing it.

"Well, Rass, what did he say? What's Dad got to say?"

"Bertie, I'll be needing to go into town shoppin' with you, if it's all right."

Bertie smiled knowingly and said, "So Dad wrote to you."

Bertie had hit on the fact to hold on to. Dad had written the letter. Well, Rass would have to grant Dad the right to his ways if he was going to demand the right for his own. The time was past for easy hating or for hoping and wishing. He wasn't a boy anymore.

He'd buy Mom that fancy teapot that had been collecting dust at Raymond's store, and Roselee ought to be ready for a new cookbook, and Mary and Sissy would be at the "no-dolls" age, so he'd best get them dolls and buy Sally perfume like Bertie's.

For Dad? A Winchester to replace his old broken-down twelve-gauge shotgun. He was sure to appreciate getting it in the middle of the winter, when there were no crops to tend. Sure, it would cost a lot, but Rass and Verge had planned out next year's crop and the money would come. He could afford it. Dad would never say that he liked the present, of course, but that was all right. He did not need Dad's words anymore to be sure of his own worth.

Rass didn't figure he would ever go around inviting Dad's criticism, but he knew that his cutting words would not go as deeply now, either. Dad and ole lady Moore and plenty of others had all been reared under a rigid system, and they were set in their ways. Well, he wasn't set, but he had stopped trying to fight against the way Dad chose to be, and that was what he wanted the present to say. Maybe Dad would not understand all the whys, but at least he'd sense the fight was over.

Maybe, Dad, you'll sort of know that this present says that I honor you. Honor you for feedin' and housin' me and for doin' the things y'thought were right, even if I didn't agree. And I honor you for the things that y'trained into me that I don't want to change, like accepting hard work and providing a livelihood for the family and making Christmas a soft time. I honor you, Dad, by not copying your faults so's they would live on after you die. A man's faults ought not to be kept rolling on down through his kids. I've got a girl now and I think things like that.

I'd never tell y'right out, though I know y'know it anyway, but I do think I know more than you do. And I don't feel bad about it like I used to. It's right for a man to improve in his kids.

Remember that one wild horse that you never could break and you had to sell him? Well, afterward, y'always acted proud when y'spoke of him, even though y'hated him. I hope you get the feeling of what I'm trying to say with this fine present, but even if y'don't, it's still necessary that I give it, and I hope you get a lot of use out of the gun.

You're mighty right, I'm coming home for Christmas, Dad. But just for Christmas!